Going To Maynooth (~~~~~ ~~~ ~~~~~~ of the Irish Peasantry)

by

William Carleton

The Echo Library 2007

Published by

The Echo Library

Echo Library
131 High St.
Teddington
Middlesex TW11 8HH

www.echo-library.com

Please report serious faults in the text to complaints@echo-library.com

ISBN 978-1-40684-223-4

GOING TO MAYNOOTH.

Young Denis O'Shaughnessy was old Denis's son; and old Denis, like many great men before him, was the son of his father and mother in particular, and a long line of respectable ancestors in general. He was, moreover, a great historian, a perplexing controversialist, deeply read in Dr. Gallagher and Pastorini, and equally profound in the history of Harry the Eighth, and Luther's partnership with the devil. Denis was a tall man, who, from his peculiar appearance, and the nature of his dress, a light drab-colored frieze, was nicknamed the Walking Pigeon-house; and truly, on seeing him at a distance, a man might naturally enough hit upon a worse comparison. He was quite straight, carried both his arms hanging by his sides, motionless and at their full length, like the pendulums of a clock that has ceased going. In his head, neck, and chest there was no muscular action visible; he walked, in fact, as if a milk-pail were upon his crown, or as if a single nod of his would put the planets out of order. But the principal cause of the similarity lay in his roundness, which resembled that of a pump, running to a point, or the pigeon-house aforesaid, which is still better.

Denis, though a large man, was but a small farmer, for he rented only eighteen acres of good land. His family, however, like himself, was large, consisting of thirteen children, among whom Denis junior stood pre-eminent. Like old Denis, he was exceedingly long-winded in argument, pedantic as the schoolmaster who taught him, and capable of taking a very comprehensive grasp of any tangible subject.

Young Denis's display of controversial talents was so remarkably precocious, that he controverted his father's statements upon all possible subjects, with a freedom from embarrassment which promised well for that most distinguished trait in a controversialist—hardihood of countenance. This delighted old Denis to the finger ends.

"Dinny, if he's spared," he would say, "will be a credit to us all yet. The sorra one of him but's as manly as anything, and as longheaded as a four-footed baste, so he is! nothing daunts or dashes him, or puts him to an amplush: but he'll look you in the face so stout an' cute, an' never redden or stumble, whether he's right or wrong, that it does one's heart good to see him. Then he has such a laning to it, you see, that the crathur 'ud ground an argument on anything, thin draw it out to a norration an' make it as clear as rock-water, besides incensing you so well into the rason of the thing, that Father Finnerty himself 'ud hardly do it betther from the althar."

The highest object of an Irish peasant's ambition is to see his son a priest. Whenever a farmer happens to have a large family, he usually destines one of them for the church, if his circumstances are at all such as can enable him to afford the boy a proper education. This youth becomes the centre in which all the affections of the family meet. He is cherished, humored in all his caprices, indulged in his boyish predilections, and raised over the heads of his brothers, independently of all personal or relative merit in himself. The consequence is, that he gradually became self-willed, proud, and arrogant, often to an offensive degree; but all this is frequently mixed up with a lofty bombast, and an undercurrent of strong disguised affection, that render his early life remarkably ludicrous and amusing. Indeed, the pranks of pedantry, the pretensions to knowledge, and the humor with which it is mostly displayed, render these scions of divinity, in their intercourse with the people until the period of preparatory education is completed, the most interesting and comical class, perhaps, to be found in the kingdom. Of these learned priestlings young Denis was undoubtedly a first-rate specimen. His father, a man of no education, was, nevertheless, as profound and unfathomable upon his favorite subjects as a philosopher; but this profundity raised him mightily in the opinion of the people, who admired him the more the less they understood him.

Now old Denis was determined that young Denis should tread in his own footsteps; and, sooth to say, young Denis possessed as bright a talent for the dark and mysterious as the father himself. No sooner had the son commenced Latin with the intention of adorning the church, than the father put him in training for controversy. For a considerable time the laurels were uniformly borne away by the veteran: but what will not learning do? Ere long the son got as far as syntax, about which time the father began to lose ground, in consequence of some ugly quotations which the son threw into his gizzard, and which unfortunately stuck there. By and by the father receded more and more, as the son advanced in his Latin and Greek, until, at length, the encounters were only resorted to for the purpose of showing off the son.

When young Denis had reached the age of sixteen or seventeen, he was looked upon by his father and his family, as well as by all their relations in general, as a prodigy. It was amusing to witness the delight with which the worthy man would call upon his son to exhibit his talents, a call to which the son instantly attended. This was usually done by commencing a mock controversy, for the gratification of some neighbor to whom the father was anxious to prove the great talents of his son. When old Denis got the young sogarth fairly in motion, he gently drew himself out of the dispute, but continued a running comment upon the son's erudition, pointed out his good things, and occasionally resumed the posture of the controversialist to reinspirit the boy if he appeared to flag.

"Dinny, abouchal, will you come up till Phadrick Murray hears you arguin' Scripthur wid myself, Dinny. Now, Phadrick, listen, but keep your tongue sayin' nothin'; just lave us to ourselves. Come up, Dinny, till you have a hate at arguin' wid myself."

"Fadher, I condimnate you at once—I condimnate you as being a most ungrammatical ould man, an' not fit to argue wid any one that knows Murray's English Grammar, an' more espaciously the three concords of Lily's Latin one; that is the cognation between the nominative case and the verb, the consanguinity between the substantive and the adjective, and the blood-relationship that irritates between the relative and the antecedent."

"I tould you, Phadrick!! There's the boy that can rattle off the high English, and the larned Latin, jist as if he was born wid an English Dictionary in one cheek, a Latin Neksuggawn in the other, an Doctor Gallagher's Irish Sarmons nately on the top of his tongue between the two."

"Fadher, but that unfortunately I am afflicted wid modesty, I'd blush crocus for your ignorance, as Virgil asserts in his Bucolics, *ut Virgilius ait in Bucolids*; and as Horatius, a book that I'm well acquainted wid, says in another place, *Huc pertinent verba*, says he, *commodandi, comparandi, dandi, prornittendi, soluendi imperandi nuntiandi, fidendi, obsequendi, minandi irascendi, et iis contraria.*"

"That's a good boy, Dinny; but why would you blush for my ignorance, avourneen? Take care of yourself now an' spake deep, for I'll outargue you at the heel o' the hunt, cute as you are."

"Why do I blush for your ignorance, is it? Why thin, I'm sure I have sound rasons for it; only think of the gross persivarance wid which you call that larned work, the Lexicon in Greek, a neck-suggan. Fadher, never, attempt to argue or display your ignorance wid me again. But, moreover, I can probate you to be an ungrammatical man from your own modus of argument."

"Go an, avourneen. Phadrick!!"

"I'm listenin'. The sorra's no match for his cuteness, an' one's puzzled to think where he can get it all."

"Why, you don't know at all what I could do by larnin'. It would be no throuble to me to divide myself into two halves, an' argue the one agin the other."

"You would, in throth, Dinny."

"Ay, father, or cut myself acrass, an' dispute my head, maybe, agin my heels."

"Throth, would you!"

"Or practise logic wid my right hand, and bate that agin wid my left."

"The sarra lie in it."

"Or read the Greek Tistament wid my right eye, an thranslate it at the same time wid my left, according to the Greek an' English sides of my face, wid my tongue constrein' into Irish, unknownst to both o' them."

"Why, Denis, he must have a head like a bell to be able to get into things."

"Throth an' he has that, an' 'ill make a noise in conthroversy yet, if he lives. Now, Dinny, let us have a hate at histhory."

"A hate at histhory?—wid all my heart; but before we begin, I tell you that I'll confound you precipitately; for you see, if you bate me in the English, I'll scarify you wid Latin, and give you a bang or two of Greek into the bargain. Och! I wish you'd hear the sackin' I gave Tom Reilly the other day; rubbed him down, as the masther says, wid a Greek towel, an' whenever I complimented him with the loan of a cut on the head, I always gave him a plaster of Latin to heal it; but the sorra worse healin' flesh in the world than Tom's is for the Latin, so I bruised a few Greek roots and laid them to his caput so nate, that you'd laugh to see him. Well is it histhory we are to begin wid? If it is, come on—advance. I'm ready for you—in protection—wid my guards up."

"Ha, ha, ha! Well, if he isn't the drollest crathur, an' so cute! But now for the histhory. Can you prove to me, upon a clear foundation, the differ atween black an' white, or prove that Phadrick Murray here, long life to him, is an ass? Now, Phadrick, listen, for you must decide betune us."

"Orra, have you no other larnin' than that to argue upon? Sure if you call upon me to decide, I must give it agin Dinny. Why my judgment won't be worth a hap'orth, if he makes an ass of me!"

"What matther how you decide, man alive, if he proves you to be one; sure that is all we want. Never heed shakin' your head—listen an' it will be well worth your while. Why, man, you'll know more nor you ever knew or suspected before, when he proves you to be an ass."

"In the first place, fadher, you're ungrammatical in one word; instead of sayin' 'prove,' always say probate, or probe; the word is descended, that is, the ancisthor of it, is probo, a deep Greek word—probo, probas, prob-ass, that is to say, I'm to probe Phadrick here to be an ass. Now, do you see how pat I brought that in? That's the way, Phadrick, I chastise my fadher with the languages."

"In throth it is; go an avick. Phadrick!"

"I'm listenin'."

"Phadrick, do you know the differ atween black an' white'?"

"Atween black an' white? Hut, gorsoon, to be sure I do."

"Well, an' what might it be, Phadrick, my larned Athiop? What might it be, I negotiate?"

"Why, thin, the differ atween them is this, Dinny, that black is—let me see—why—that black is not red—nor yellow—nor brown—nor green—nor purple—not cut-beard—nor a heather color—nor a grog-ram"—

"Nor a white?"

"Surely, Dinny, not a white, abouchal; don't think to come over me that way."

"But I want to know what color it is, most larned sager."

"All rasonable, Dinny, Why, thin, black is—let me see—hut, death alive!—it's—a—a—why, it's black, an' that's all I can say about it; yes, faix, I can—black is the color of Father Curtis's coat."

"An' what color is that, Phadrick?"

"Why, it's black, to be sure."

"Well, now, what color is white, Phadrick?"

"Why, it's a snow-color: for all the world the color of snow."

"White is?"

"Ay, is it."

"The dear help your head, Phadrick, if that's all you know about snow. In England, man, snow is an Oxford gray, an' in Scotland, a pepper an' salt, an' sometimes a cut-beard, when they get a hard winther. I found that much in the Greek, any way, Phadrick. Thry agin, you imigrant, I'll give you another chance—what color is white?"

"Why, thin, it's—white—an' nothin' else. The sorra one but you'd puzzle a saint wid your long-headed screwtations from books."

"So, Phadrick, your preamble is, that white is white, an' black is black?"

"Asy avick. I said, sure enough, that white is white; but the black I deny—I said it was the color of Father Curtis's black coat."

"Oh, you barbarian of the world, how I scorn your profundity an' emotions! You're a disgrace to the human sex by your superciliousness of knowledge, an' your various quotations of ignorance. Ignorantia, Phadrick, is your date an' superscription. Now, stretch out your ears, till I probate, or probe to you the differ atween black an' white."

"Phadrick!!" said the father.

"I'm listenin'."

"Now, Phadrick, here's the griddle, an' here's a clane plate. Do you see them here beside one another?"

"I'm lookin' at them."

"Now, shut your eyes."

"Is that your way, Denis, of judgin' colors?"

"Shut your eyes, I say, till I give you ocular demonstration of the differ atween these two respectable colors."

"Well, they're shut."

"An' keep them so. Now, what differ do you see atween them?"

"The sorra taste, man alive; I never seen anything in my whole life so clearly of a color as they are both this minute."

"Don't you see now, Phadrick, that there's not the smallest taste o' differ in them, an' that's accordin' to Euclid."

"Sure enough, I see the divil a taste o' differ atween the two."

"Well, Phadrick, that's the point settled. There's no discrimination at all atween black an' white. They're both of the same color—so long as you keep your eyes shut."

"But if a man happens to open his eyes, Dinny?"

"He has no right to open them, Phadrick, if he wants to prove the truth of a thing. I should have said probe—but it does not significate."

"The heavens mark you to grace, Dinny. You did that in brave style. Phadrick, ahagur, he'll make the darlin' of an arguer whin he gets the robes an him."

"I don't deny that; he'll be aquil to the best o' thim: still, Denis, I'd rather, whin I want to pronounce upon colors, that he'd let me keep my eyes open."

"Ay, but he did it out o' the books, man alive; an' there's no goin' beyant thim. Sure he could prove it out of the Divinity, if you went to that. An' what is still more, he could, by shuttin' your eyes, in the same way prove black to be white, an' white black, jist as asy."

"Surely myself doesn't doubt it. I suppose, by shuttin' my eyes, the same lad could prove anything to me."

"But, Dinny, avourneen, you didn't prove Phadrick to be an ass yit. Will you do that by histhory, too, Dinny, or by the norrations of Illocution?"

"Father, I'm surprised at your gross imperception. Why, man, if you were not a *rara avis* of somnolency, a man of most frolicsome determinations, you'd be able to see that I've proved Phadrick to be an ass already."

"Throth, I deny that you did; there wasn't a word about my bein' an ass, in the last discoorse. It was all upon the differ atween black an' white."

"Oh, how I scorn your gravity, man! *Ignorantia*, as I said, is your date an' superscription; an' when you die, you ought to go an' engage a stone-cutter to carve you a headstone, an' make him write on it, *Hic jacet Ignorantius Redivicus*. An' the translation of that is, accordin' to Publius Virgilius Maro—'here lies a quadruped who didn't know the differ atween black an' white.'"

"Well, by the livin', Dinny, I dunna where you get all this deep readin'."

"Sure he gets it all in the Dixonary."

"Bedad, that Dixonary must be a fine book entirely, to thim that undherstand it."

"But, Dinny, will you tell Phadrick the Case of Conscience atween Barny Branagan's two goats an' Parra Ghastha's mare?"

"Fadher, if you were a grammarian, I'd castigate your incompatability as it desarves—I'd lay the scourge o' syntax upon you, as no man ever got it since the invintion o' the nine parts of speech. By what rule of logic can you say that aither Barny Branagan's goats or Parra Ghastha's mare had a conscience? I tell you it wasn't they had the conscience, but the divine who decided the difficulty. Phadrick, lie down till I illusthrate."

"How is that, Dinny? I can hear you sittin'."

"Lie down, you reptile, or I shall decline the narration altogether."

"Arra, lie down, Phadrick; sure he only wants to show you the rason o' the thing."

"Well, well; I'm down. Now Dinny, don't let your feet be too larned, if you plase."

"Silence!—*taceto!* you reptile. Now, Phadrick, here, on this side o' you, lies Barny Branagan's field; an' there, on that side, lies a field of Parra Ghastha's; you're the ditch o' mud betuxt them."

"The ditch o' mud! Faix that's dacent!"

"Now here, on Barny Branagan's side, feeds Parra Ghastha's mare; an' there, on Parra Ghastha's side, feed Barny Branagan's goats. Do you comprehend? Do you insinuate?"

"I do—I do. Death alive! there's no use in punchin' my sides wid your feet that way."

"Well, get up now an' set your ears."

"Now listen to him, Phadrick!"

"It was one night in winter, when all nature shone in the nocturnal beauty of tenebrosity: the sun had set about three hours before; an', accordin' to the best logicians, there was a dearth of light. It's the general opinion of philosophers— that is, of the soundest o' them—that when the sun is down the moon an' stars are usually up; an' so they were on the night that I'm narratin' about. The moon was, wid great respect to her character, night-walkin' in the sky; and the stars vegetated in celestial genuflexion around her. Nature, Phadrick, was in great state; the earth was undher our feet, an' the sky above us. The frost, too, was hard, Phadrick, the air keen, an' the grass tendher. All things were enrobed wid verisimilitude an' scrupulosity. In this manner was the terraqueous part of our system, when Parra Ghastha's mare, after havin' taken a cowld collation on Barny Branagan's grass, was returnin' to her master's side o' the merin; an' Barny Branagan's goats, havin' tasted the sweets of Parra Ghastha's cabbages, were on their way acrass the said merin to their own side. Now it so happened that they met exactly at a narrow gap in the ditch behind Rosha Halpin's house. The goats, bein' coupled together, got one on each side of the rift, wid the rope that coupled them extended acrass it. The mare stood in the middle of it, so that the goats were in the way of the mare, an' the mare in the way of the goats. In the meantime they surveyed one another wid great composure, but had neither of them the politeness to stir, until Rosha Halpin came suddenly out, an' emptied a vessel of untransparent wather into the ditch. The mare, who must have been an animal endowed wid great sensibility of soul, stooped her head suddenly at the noise; an' the goats, who were equally sentimental, gave a start from nervishness. The mare, on raisin' her head, came in contact wid the cord that united the goats; an' the goats, havin' lost their commandin' position, came in contact wid the neck o' the mare. *Quid multis?* They pulled an' she pulled, an' she pulled an' they pulled, until at length the mare was compelled to practise the virtue of resignation in the ditch, wid the goats about her neck. She died by suspinsion; but the mettlesome ould crathur, wid a love of justice that did her honor, hanged the goat's in requital; for they departed this vale of tears on the mountain side along wid her, so that they had the satisfaction of dyin' a social death together.— Now, Phadrick, you quadruped, the case of conscience is, whether Parra Ghastha has a right to make restitution to Barny Branagan for the loss of his goats, or Barny Branagan to Parra Ghastha for the loss of his mare?"

"Bedad, that's a puzzler!"

"Isn't it, Phadrick? But wait till you hear how he'll clear it up! Do it for Phadrick, Dinny."

"Yis, Phadrick, I'll illusthrate your intellects by divinity. You see, Phadrick, you're to suppose me to be in the chair, as confessor. Very well,—or *valde*, in the larned languages—Parra Ghastha comes to confess to me, an' tells me that Barny Branagan wants to be paid for his goats. I tell him it's a disputed point, an that the price o' the goats must go to the church. On the other hand, Barny Branagan tells me that Parra Ghastha wishes to be paid for his mare. I say again, it's a disputed point, an' that the price o' the mare must go to the church—the amount of the proceeds to be applied in prayer towards the benefit of the parties, in the first instance, an' of the faithful in general afterwards."

"Phadrick!!!"

"Oh, that I may never, but he bates the globe!"

Denny's character is a very common one in the remote parts of Ireland, where knowledge is novelty, and where the slightest tinge of learning is looked upon with such reverence and admiration, as can be properly understood only by those who have an opportunity of witnessing it. Indeed, few circumstances prove the great moral influence which the Irish priesthood possesses over the common people more forcibly, than the extraordinary respect paid by the latter to such as are designed for the "mission." The moment the determination is made, an incipient sanctity begins, as it were, to consecrate the young priest; and a high opinion of his learning and talents to be entertained, no matter how dull he may be so far as honest nature is concerned. Whatever he says is sure to have some hidden meaning in it, that would be' highly edifying, if they themselves understood it. But their own humility comes in here to prop up his talents; and whatsoever perplexity there may be in the sense of what he utters, is immediately attributed to learning altogether beyond their depth.

Love of learning is a conspicuous principle in an Irish peasant; and in no instance is it seen to greater advantage, than when the object of it appears in the "makins of a priest." Among all a peasant's good and evil qualities, this is not the least amiable. How his eye will dance in his head with pride, when the young priest thunders out a line of Virgil or Homer, a sentence from Cicero, or a rule from Syntax! And with what complacency and affection will the father and relations of such a person, when sitting during a winter evening about the hearth, demand from him a translation of what he repeats, or a grammatical analysis, in which he must show the dependencies and relations of word upon word—the concord, the verb, the mood, the gender, and the case; into every one and all of which the learned youth enters with an air of oracular importance, and a pollysyllabicism of language that fails not in confounding them with astonishment and edification. Neither does Paddy confine himself to Latin or Greek, for his curiosity in hearing a little upon all known branches of human learning is boundless. When a lad is designed for the priesthood, he is, as if by a species of intuition, supposed to know more or less of everything—astronomy, fluxions, Hebrew, Arabic, and the black art, are subjects upon which he is frequently expected to dilate; and vanity scruples not, under the protection of their ignorance, to lead the erudite youth through what they believe to be the highest regions of imagination, or the profoundest depths of science and philosophy.

It is, indeed, in those brilliant moments, when the young priest is launching out in full glory upon some topic of which he knows not a syllable, that it would be a learned luxury to catch him. These flights, however, are very pardonable, when we consider the importance they give him in the eyes of his friends, and reflect upon that lofty and contemptuous pride, and those delectable sensations which the appearance of superior knowledge gives to the pedant, whether raw or trained, high or low, in this profession or the other. It matters little that such a feeling dilates the vanity in proportion to the absence of real knowledge or good sense: it is not real, but affected knowledge, we are writing about. Pride is confined to no condition; nor is the juvenile pedantry of a youth upon the hob of an Irish chimney-corner much different from the pride which sits upon the brow of a worthy Lord Mayor, freshly knighted, lolling with strained dignity beside his honorable brother, the mace, during a city procession; or of a Lady Mayoress, when she reads upon a dead wall her own name flaming in yellow capitals, at the head of a subscription ball; or, what is better still, the contemptuous glance which, while about to open the said ball, her ladyship throws at that poor creature—the Sheriff's wife.

In addition, however, to the enjoyment of this assumption of profound learning which characterizes the young priest, a different spirit, considerably more practical, often induces him to hook in other motives. The learning of Denis O'Shaughnessy, for instance, blazed with peculiar lustre whenever he felt himself out at elbows; for the logic with which he was able to prove the connection between his erudition and a woollen-draper's shop, was, like the ignorance of those who are to be saved, invincible. Whenever his father considered a display of the son's powers in controversy to be *capital*, Denis, who knew the *mollia tempora fandi*, applied to him for a hat. Whenever he drew a heretic, as a person who will be found hereafter without the wedding garment, and clinched the argument with half a dozen quotations from syntax or Greek grammar, he uniformly came down upon the father for a coat, the cloth of which was finer in proportion to the web of logic he wove during the disputation. Whenever he seated himself in the chair of rhetoric, or gave an edifying homily on prayer, with such eloquence as rendered the father's admiration altogether inexpressible, he applied for a pair of smallclothes; and if, in the excursiveness of his vigorous imagination he travelled anywhere beyond the bounds of common sense, he was certain to secure a pair of shoes.

This, of course, did not escape the satirical observation of the neighbors, who commented upon the circumstance with that good humor which renders their mother-wit so pleasant and spicy. The scenes where many of these displays took place, varied according to the occurrence of those usual incidents which diversify country life. Sometimes old Denis's hearth was selected; at others, a neighboring wakehouse, and not unfrequently the chapel-green, where, surrounded by a crowd of eager listeners, the young priest and his Latin would succeed in throwing the hedge-schoolmaster and his problems completely into the shade.

The father's pride, on these occasions, always prompted him to become the aggressor; but he only did this to draw out the talents of his son to more advantage. Never was man foiled with less regret than old Denis; nor did ever man more bitterly repent those little touches of vanity, which, sometimes induced him, when an opportunity of prostrating Denny arrived, to show what he could have done, by giving the son's argument an unexpected brainblow. These accidental defeats always brought the son! more than he lost by them; for the father usually made him a peace-offering in the shape of pocket-money, books, or clothes. The great amusement of the peasantry around the chapel-green of a Sunday, was to hear the father and son engaged in argument; and so simple was the character of both, that their acquaintances declared, they could know by the state of young Denis's coat, and the swaggering grasp with which old Denis held his staff, that an encounter was about to take place.

"Young O'Shaughnessy's gettin' bare," they would observe; "there'll be hard arguin' till he gets the clothes. He's puttin' in for a black coat now, he's so grave. Go on, Denny," they would say again: "more power an' a dacenter sleeve to your elbow. Stick to him!—very good!—that's a clincher!—you're gone beyond the skirts, Denny!—let him pocket that larnin'. Dinis, you're bate, body and slaves!!¹—you're no match for the gorsoon, Dinis. Good agin, abouchal!—that's puttin' the collar on it!"—And so on, varying the phrase according to the whim of the moment.

Nothing gave the father greater pleasure than these observations, although the affected earnestness with which he encountered the son, and his pretended indignation at those who affirmed him to have been beaten, were highly amusing to the bystanders.

Such discussions were considered highly edifying and instructive by them, and they were sometimes at a loss whether to give the palm of ingenuity and eloquence to the father or Denny. The reader, however, must not suppose that the contemptuous expressions scattered over Denny's rhetorical flourishes; when discussing these points with his father, implied want of reverence or affection—far from it. On the contrary, the father always liked him the better for them, inasmuch as they proved Denny's vast superiority over himself. They were, therefore, only the licenses and embellishments of discussion, tolerated and encouraged by him to whom they were applied.

Denny at length shot up to the stature of a young man, probably about eighteen; and during the two last years of his school studies he presented a considerable, if not a decidedly marked change in his character and external appearance. His pride became more haughty, and the consciousness of his learning, and of the influence annexed to the profession for which he was intended, put itself forth with less discussion, but more energy. His manners and attitude became constrained; the expression of his face began to darken, and to mould itself into a stiff, gloomy formality, that was strongly calculated to conceal the natural traits of his character. His dress, too, had undergone a great improvement; for instead of wearing shop blue or brown, he wore good black broad-cloth, had a watch in his fob, a respectable hat, and finer linen.

This change, now necessary in consequence of his semiclerical character, influenced him through every relation of life. His nearest friends, whilst their pride in him increased, fell off to a more respectful distance; and his deportment, so far from being that of a good-humored Bobadil of polemics and pedantry upon all known and unknown subjects, became silent and solemn, chequered only during the moments of family conviviality by an excessive flow of that pleasant and still incomprehensible learning for the possession of which he had so honestly earned himself a character. Much of his pedantry was now lopped off, it is true, because the pride of his station prevented him from entering into discussions with the people. It cost him, however, some trouble to overcome his early tendencies; nor, after all, can it be affirmed that he altogether succeeded in eradicating them. Many a grave shrug, and solemn wink, and formal nod, had he to answer for, when his foot touched the debatable land of controversy. Though contrary to the keeping and dignity of his position in life,

---

¹ altogether; completely

yet did honest Denny then get desperately significant, and his face amazingly argumentative. Many a pretender has he fairly annihilated by a single smile of contempt that contained more logic than a long argument from another man. In fact, the whole host of rhetorical figures seemed breaking out of his face. By a solitary glance of his eye he could look a man into a dilemma, and practise a *sorites*, or a homemade syllogism, by the various shiftings of his countenance, as clearly as if he had risen to the full flight of his former bombast. He had, in short, a *prima facie* disposition to controversy; his nose was set upon his face in a kind of firm defiance against infidels, heretics, and excommunicated persons; and when it curled with contempt of another, or with pride in the power that slumbered in itself, it seemed to give the face from which it projected, and the world at large, the assurance of a controversialist. Nor did his negative talents rest here: a twist of his mouth to the right or left ear, was nicely shaded away into a negative or affirmative, according as he intended it should be taken; and when he used his pocket-handkerchief, he was certain, though without uttering a syllable, to silence his opponent, so contemptuously did his intonations rout the arguments brought against him. The significance and force of all these was heightened by the mystery in which they were wrapped; for whenever unbending decorum constrained him to decline the challenges of the ignorant, with whom discussion would now be degradation, what could he do to soothe his vanity, except, as the poet says, with folded arms and a shaking of the head to exclaim—"*Well, well we know;* or, *if we could, and if we would;* or, *if we list to speak*; or, *there be an if they might;*" which left the imaginations of his hearers at liberty to conceive more fully of those powers which his modesty declined exhibiting. For some time before he got absolutely and finally into black, even his father gave up his accustomed argument in despair. The son had become an adept in all the intricacies and obscurities of Latin, and literally overwhelmed the old man with small inundations of that language, which though, like all inundations, rather muddy, yet were they quite sufficient to sweep the worthy veteran before them.

Young Denis O'Shaughnessy was now pretty nearly finished at school, that is to say, almost fit for Maynooth; his studies, though higher, were less assiduous; his leisure was consequently greater; and it is well known, that a person of his character is never asked to work, except it be his own pleasure to labor a day or two, by way of amusement. He might now be seen walking of a warm day along the shady sides of the hedges, with a book in his hand, or stretched listlessly upon the grass, at study; or sauntering about among the neighboring workmen, with his forefinger between the leaves of his book, a monument of learning and industry.

It is not to be supposed, however, that Denis, who was an Irishman of eighteen, handsome and well made, could be altogether insensible to female beauty, and seductive charms of the sex. During his easy saunterings—or, as the Scotch say, "daunerings"—along the roads and about the green hedges, it often happened that he met a neighbor's daughter; and Denis, who, as a young gentleman of breeding, was bound to be courteous, could not do less than accost her with becoming urbanity.

"Good-mornin', Miss Norah," we will suppose him to say, when meeting a good-looking arch girl of his acquaintance.

"Good-morrow, Mr. O'Shaughnessy. I hope you're well, sir."

"Indeed I am, at present, in superlatively ecclesiastical health, Miss Norah. I hope all your family are well?"

"All very well, I thank you, sir, barrin' myself."

"An' pray what's the matther wid you, Miss Norah? I hope" (with an exceeding grave but complacent smile) "you're not affected wid the amorous passion of love?"

"Oh, that 'ud be tellin', Mr. O'Shaughnessy! But supposin' I am, what ought I to do?"

"That's really a profound question, Miss Norah. But though I cannot tell you what to do, I can tell you what I think."

"An' what is that, sir?"

"Why, Miss Norah, that he who is so beatified as to secure you in the matrimonial paction—*compactum* it is in the larned languages—in other words—to condescend to your capacity—he who is married to you will be a happy man. There is a juvenility about your eyes, and an efflorescence of amaranthine odoriferousness about your cheeks and breath that are enough to communicate the centrifugal motion to any brain adorned with the slightest modicum of sentiment."

"He who marries me will be a happy man!" she exclaimed, repeating these expressions, probably because they were the only words she understood. "I hope so, Misther O'Shaughnessy. But, sure enough, who'd expect to hear sich soft talk from the makins of a priest? Very well, sir! Upon my word I'll be tellin' Father Finnerty that you do be spakin' up to the girls!—Now!!"

"No, no, Miss Norah; you wouldn't do that merely for my sayin' that you're the handsomest girl in the parish. Father Finnerty himself might say as much, for it would be nothing but veracity—nothing but truth, Miss Norah."

"Ah! but he wouldn't be pattin' me on the cheek! Be asy, Mr. O'Shaughnessy; there's Darby Brady lookin' at you, an' he'll be tellin'!"

"Where?" said Denis, starting.

The girl replied only by an arch laugh.

"Upon my classicality, Miss Norah, you're a rogue; there's nobody lookin', you seraphim!"

"Then there's a pair of us rogues, Misther Dinis."

"No, no, Miss Norah; I was only feeling your cheek as a philosophical experiment. Philosophers often do it, in order to make out an hypothesis."

"Misther Dinis, if I'm not marrid till you're a priest, won't you say the words for me for nothing?"

"So long as you ask it wid such a brilliant smiled Miss Norah, do you think that any educated young man who has read about beauty an' sentimentality in books, could refuse you? But you know, Miss Norah, that the clergyman who marries a couple has always the right of kissing the bride. Now I wouldn't claim my right then; but it might be possible by a present compromise to—to———. What would you think, for instance, to give me that now?"

"To give you what?"

"Why the———indeed it's but a slight recompense, the—k—— the salutation—the kiss. You know what tasting the head means?"

"Faix, Misther Dinis, you're a great rogue. Who'd think it indeed? Sure enough, they say smooth water runs deep! Why one 'ud suppose butther wouldn't melt in your mouth to look at you; an' yet you want to be toyin' wid the girls! Indeed an' faix, it's a great shame for the likes o' you, that's bint on Maynooth, to be thinkin' of coortin' at all. But wait! Upon my word, I'll have a fine story agin you, plase goodness!"

This latter threat the mischievous girl threw out with a grave face, in order to bring Denis into a more ridiculous dilemma; for she saw clearly that he labored under a heavy struggle between timidity and gallantry. The ruse succeeded. Denis immediately changed his tone, and composed his face into a grave admonitory aspect, nearly equal to a homily on prudence and good conduct.

"Miss Norah," said he, "perhaps I acted wrong in carrying my trial of your disposition too far. It's a thing, however, which we who are intended for the church are ordered to do, that we may be able to make out what are called in this very book you see wid me, cases of conscience. But the task is now over, Miss Norah; and, in requital for your extreme good nature, I am bound to administer to you a slight lecture on decorum.

"In the first place, attend your duties regularly. I will soon be goin' to Maynooth; an' as you are one of the girls for whom I have the greatest regard, I will expect on my return to hear a good account of you. It is possible that you'll be introduced in my absence to the honors of matrimony; but even so, I know that peace, an' taciturnity, an' submission will be your most signal qualifications. You will then be in a situation equal to that of a Roman matron. As for us, Miss Norah, we are subject to the dilapidations of occasional elevation. The ambrosia of sentiment lies in our path. We care not for the terrestrialities of life, when separated from the great principle of the poet—

'*Omnia vincit amor, et nos cedamus amori.*'

That's Hebrew, Miss Norah!"

"They say you know a power of larnin', Misther Dinis."

"Yes, I know the seven languages; but what is all that compared to the cardinal virtues. This world is a mere bird of passage, Miss Norali; and it behooves us to be ever on the wing for futurity and premeditation. Now, will you remember the excellent moral advice I have given you?"

"Indeed I will, sir," replied the roguish minx, tripping away; "particularly that you promised to marry me for nothin' if I'd give you a kiss!"

"Give up everything like levity, Miss Norah. Attend your du—"

"You're a fool, Misther O'Shaughnessy! Why didn't you take the kiss, an' spare the king's English?"

On making this observation she redoubled her pace, and left Denis now perfectly sensible that he was a proper subject for her mirth. He turned about, and called after her—

"Had I known that you were only in jocosity, Miss Nora, upon my classicality, I'd have given you the k———."

He now perceived that she was beyond hearing, and that it was unnecessary to finish the sentence.

These accidental meetings between Denis and the pretty daughters of the neighboring farmers were, somehow, very frequent. Our hero, however, was always extremely judicious in tempering his gallantry and moral advice to his young female acquaintances. In the beginning of the conversation he was sly and complimentary, afterwards he became more insinuating, then more direct in his praises of their beauty; but as his timidity on the point of character was known, the mischief-loving girls uniformly ended with a threat of exposing him to the priest, to his friends, or to the neighbors, as the whim directed them. This brought him back to his morality again; he immediately commenced an exhortation touching their religious duties, thus hoping to cover, by a trait more becoming his future destination, the little harmless badinage in which he had indulged.

The girls themselves frequently made him the topic of conversation, a proof that he was not altogether indifferent to them. In these little conclaves he came very well off. Among them all it was admitted "that there was a rogue in his coat;" but this was by no means uttered in a tone of voice that betrayed any disrelish to him. On the contrary, they often said—and many of them with an involuntary sigh—that "he was too purty to be made a priest of;" others, that "it was a pity to make a priest of so fine a young man;" others, again, that "if he must be a priest, the colleens would be all flockin' to hear his sarmons." There was one, however, among them who never mentioned him either in praise or censure; but the rapid changes of her expressive countenance gave strong indications to an observing eye that his name, person, and future prospects were capable of exciting a deep and intense interest in her heart.

At length he began to appear on horseback; and as he had hitherto been in the habit of taking that exercise bare-backed, now he was resolved to get into a saddle, and ride like a gentleman. Henceforth he might be seen mounted upon one of his father's horses, quite erect, and with but one spur, which was, in fact, the only spur, except the whiskey bottle, that had been in the family for three generations. This was used, he declared, for no other purpose in life than that of "stimulating the animal to the true clerical trot."

From the moment he became a mounted man he assumed an air of less equivocal command in the family; and not only to his own relations was this authority manifested, but to his more distant acquaintances, and, in short, to the whole parish. The people now began to touch their hats to him, which act of respect he returned as much in imitation of the parish priest as possible. They also began to ask him what o'clock it was, and Denis, with a peculiar condescension, balanced still with becoming dignity, stopped, pulled out his watch, and told the hour, after which he held it for a few seconds to his ear with an experienced air, then put it in a dignified manner in his fob, touched the horse with the solitary spur, put himself more erect, and proceeded with—as he himself used to say, when condemning the pride of the curate—"all the lordliness of the parochial priest."

The notions which the peasantry entertain of a priest's learning are as extravagant as they are amusing, and such, indeed, as would be too much for the pedantic vanity inseparable from a half-educated man to disclaim. The people are sufficiently reasonable, however, to admit gradations in the extent of knowledge acquired by their pastors; but some of the figures and illustrations which they use in estimating their comparative merits are highly ludicrous. I remember a young man, who, at the age of twenty-two, set about preparing himself for the church. He lived in the bosom of a mountain, whose rugged breast he cultivated with a strength proportioned to the difficulty of subduing it. He was a powerful young fellow, quiet and inoffensive in his manners, and possessed of great natural talents. It was upon a Monday morning, in the month of June, that the school-room door opened a foot and a half wider than usual, and a huge, colossal figure stalked in, with a kind of bashful laugh upon his countenance, as if conscious of the disproportion betwixt his immense size and that of the other schoolboys. His figure, without a syllable of exaggeration, was precisely such as I am about to describe. His height six feet, his shoulders of an enormous breadth, his head red as fire; his body-coat made after the manner of his grandfather's—the skirts of it being near his heels—and the buttons behind little less than eighteen inches asunder. The pockets were cut so low, that when he stretched his arm to its full length, his fingers could not get further than the flaps; the breast of it was about nine inches longer than was necessary, so that when he buttoned it, he appeared all body. He wore no cravat, nor was his shirt-collar either pinned or buttoned, but lay open as if to disclose an immense neck and chest scorched by the sun into a rich and healthy scarlet. His chin was covered with a sole of red-dry bristles, that appeared to have been clipped about a fortnight before; and as he wore neither shoe nor stocking, he exhibited a pair of legs to which Rob Roy's were drumsticks. They gave proof of powerful strength, and the thick fell of bristly hair with which they were covered argued an amazing hardihood of constitution and tremendous physical energy.

"Sure, Masther, I'm comin' to school to you!" were the first words he uttered.

Now there ran beneath the master's solemnity of manner a broad but shallow under-current of humor, which agreed but poorly with his pompous display of learning. On this occasion his struggle to retain the grave and overcome the ludicrous was unavailing. The startling fact thus uncouthly announced by so grotesque a candidate for classical knowledge occasioned him to receive the intelligence with more mirth than was consistent with good breeding. His pupils, too, who were hitherto afraid to laugh aloud, on observing his countenance dilate into an expression of laughter which he could not conceal, made the roof of the house ring with their mirth.

"Silence, gintlemen," said he; "*legite, perlegite, et relegite*—study, gintlemen, study—pluck the tree of knowledge, I say, while the fruit is in season. Denny O'Shaughnessy, what are you facetious for? *Quid rides, Dionysi* And so, Pether—is Pettier your pronomen—quo nomine gowdes? Silence, boys!—perhaps he was at Latin before, and we'll try him—*quo nomine gowdes, Pethre?*"

A stare of awkward perplexity was the only reply he could get from the colossus he addressed.

"And so you're fished up from the Streights[2] at last, Pether?"

"Sir, my name's not Pether. My father's name is Paddy Doorish, but my own is Franky. I was born in Lisnagh; but we lived double as long as I can mind in the Mountain Bar."

"And, Franky, what put Latin into your head?"

"There was no Latin put into my head; I'm comin' to you for that."

"And, you graceful sprig of juvenility, have you the conscience to think that I'd undhertake to fill what you carry on your showlders on the same terms that I'd take for replenishing the head of a rasonable youth? Would you be so unjust in all the principles of correct erudition as to expect that, my worthy Man-mountain?"

"I don't expect it," said Frank; "all that's in your head wouldn't fill the corner of mine, if you go accordin' to size; but I'll pay you for tachin' me as much as you know yourself, an' the more I larn the less pains you'll have wid me."

Franky, however, made an amazing progress—so very rapid, indeed, that in about three years from that day he found himself in Maynooth, and in three years more was an active curate, to whom that very teacher appeared as slavishly submissive as if he had never ridiculed his vulgarity or ungainly dimensions. Poor Frank, however, in consequence of the rapid progress he made, and of the very short interval which elapsed from the period of his commencing Latin until that of his ordination, was assigned by the people the lowest grade in learning. The term used to designate the rank which they supposed him to hold, was both humorous and expressive.

"Franky," they would say, "is no finished priest in the larnin'; he's but a *scowdher*."

Now a *scowdher* is an oaten cake laid upon a pair of tongs placed over the greeshaugh, or embers, that are spread out for the purpose of baking it. In a few minutes the side first laid down is scorched: it is then turned, and the other side is also scorched; so that it has the appearance of being baked, though it is actually quite raw within. It is a homely, but an exceedingly apt illustration, when applied to such men as Frank.

"Poor Frank," they would observe, "is but a *scowdher*—the sign of the tongs—No. 11, is upon him; so that it is asy known he never was laid to the

---

[2] Alluding to the Colossus of Rhodes

muddha arran,"[3]—that is to say, properly baked—or duly and thoroughly educated.

Denis, however, to resume more directly the thread of our narrative, on finding himself mounted, took an inveterate prejudice against walking. There was something, he thought, far more dignified in riding than in pacing slowly upon the earth, like a common man who had not the justification of Latin and Greek for becoming an equestrian. Besides this accomplishment, there were also many other habits to be broken off, and more genteel ones to be adopted in their place. These were all suggested by his rising pride; and, in sooth, they smacked strongly of that adroitness with which the Irish priest, and every priest, contrives to accomplish the purpose of feeding well through the ostensible medium of a different motive.

He accordingly took his father aside one morning, after he had eaten a more meagre breakfast that usual, and, after licking his lips, addressed him in these words:—

"I think, father, that upon considerating the consequence to which I am now entitled, and the degree of respectability which, in my own person—*in propria persona*—I communicate to the vulgarians with whom I am connected—I call them vulgarians from no derogatory motive; but you will concede yourself, that they are ignorant of the larned languages, an' consequently, though dacent enough, still, in reference to Latin and Greek, but vulgarians. Well! *Quid multis?*—I say, that taking all these things into speculation, looking at them—*veluti in speculum*—it is neither dacent nor becoming that I should ate in the manner I have done, as vulgarly as themselves—that I should ate, I say, any longer, without knife and fork. Neither, I announce, shall I in future drink my milk any longer, as I have with all humility done hitherto, out of a noggin; nor continue to disrobe, my potatoes any longer without a becoming instrument. I must also have better viands to consume. You are not to be ininformed that I am in that situation of life, in which, from my education and other accomplishments, I must be estimated as duly qualified to ate beef and mutton instead of bacon, an' to have my *tay* breakfast instead of stirabout, which, in polite society, is designated porridge. You know yourself, and must acknowledge, that I'm soon likely to confer distinction and preeminence upon the poor illiterate, but honest creatures, with whom I am associated in the bonds of blood-relationship. If I were a dunce, or a booby, or a leather head, the case might be different; but you yourself are well acquainted with my talents of logic and conthroversy; an' I have sound rasons and good authority, which I could quote, if necessary, for proving that nothing increases the weight of the brain, and accelerates to gravity and solidity more than good feeding. Pay attention, therefore, to my words, for I expect that they will be duly observed:—buy me a

---

[3] The *Muddha Arran* is literally "the bread stick," a term in opposition to the *scowdher*. It is a forked stick with three legs, that stands opposite the fire, and supports the cake, which is placed on the edge until it is gradually baked. The Scowdher is, for the most part, made in cases of hurry.

knife and fork; and when I get them, it's not to lay them past to rust, you consave. The beef and mutton must follow; and in future I'm resolved to have my *tay* breakfast. There are geese, and turkeys, and pullets enough about the yard, and I am bent on accomplishing myself in the art of carving them. I'm not the man now to be placed among the other riff-raff of the family over a basket of potatoes, wid a black clerical coat upon me, and a noggin of milk under my arm! I tell you the system must be changed: the schoolmaster is abroad, and I'll tolerate such vulgarity no longer. Now saddle the horse till I ride across the bog to Pether Rafferty's Station, where I'm to sarve mass; plase heaven, I'll soon be able to say one myself, and give you all a lift in spirituals—ehem!"

"Throth, Dinny, I b'lieve you're right, avick; and——"

"Vick me no longer, father—that's another thing I forgot. It's full time that I should be sirred; and if my own relations won't call me Sir instead of Dinny, it's hardly to be expected that strangers will do it. I wish to goodness you had never stigmatized me wid so vulgar an epithet as Dinny. The proper word is Dionysius; and, in future, I'll expect to be called Misther Dionysius."

"Sure, I or your mother needn't be sirrin' you, Dinny?"

"I haven't made up my mind as to whether I'll demand that proof of my respectability from you and my mother, or not; but on this I'm immovable, that instead of Dinny, you must, as I said, designate me Dionysius."

"Well, well, avourneen, I suppose only it's right you wouldn't be axin' us; but I'm sure your poor mother will never be able to get her tongue about Dionnisis, it's so long and larned a word."

"It is a larned word, no doubt; but she must persevere until she's able to masther it. I wouldn't for three tenpennies that the priest would hear one of you call me Dinny; it would degradate me very much in his estimation. At all events, if my mother cannot manage the orthography of Dionysius, let it be Denis, or anything but that signature of vulgarity, Dinny. Now, father, you won't neglect to revale what I've ordered to the family?"

"No, indeed, I will not, avick—I mane—Dionnisis, avourneen—I'll tell them everything as you ordhered; but as to Dionnisis, I'm cock sure that poor Mave will never be able to get her ould tongue about so newfangled a piece of larnin' as that is. Well, well, this knowledge bates the world!"

When the horse was saddled, and Dionysius on his way with all due pomp to the Station, old Denis broke the matter to his wife.

"Mave, achora," said he, "I have sthrange news to tell you: sure Dionnisis is goin' to make himself a gintleman."

"Sure what?"

"Dionnisis, our son Dionnisis, is goin' to make himself a gintleman; he'll ate no longer widout a knife and fork."

"Saints about us!" exclaimed Mave, rising and looking with alarm into her husband's face—"saints about us, Denis, what is it ails you? Sure there would be nothin' wrong wid you about the head, Denis? or maybe it's a touch of a faver you've got, out riddling that corn bare-headed, yistherday? I remember the time my Aunt Bridget tuck the scarlet faver, she begun to rave and spake foolish in the same way."

"Why, woman, if your Aunt Bridget had a faver made up of all the colors in the rainbow, I tell you I'm spakin' sinse! Our son Dionnisis proved himself a gintleman out in the garden wid me about an hour ago."

"I suppose so, Denis," she replied, humoring' him, for she was still doubly convinced that he labored under some incipient malady, if not under actual insanity; "an' what son is this, Dinny? I've never heard of him before."

"Our son Denis, woman alive! You must know he's not to be called Dinny or Dinis any more, but Dionnisis; he's to begin atin' wid a knife an' fork to-morrow; we must get him beef and mutton, and a *tay* breakfast. He say's it's not fair play in any one that's so deep read in the larnin' as he is, to ate like a vulgarian, or to peel his phaties wid his fingers, an' him knows so much Latin an' Greek; an' my sowl to happiness but he'll stick to the gintlemanly way of livin', so far as the beef, an' mutton, and tay is consamed."

"He will! An', Dinis O'Shaughnessy, who has a betther right to turn gintleman, nor the gorsoon that studied for that! Isn't it proud you ought to be that he has the spirit to think of sich things?"

"I'll engage, Mave, on that point you'll find him spirited enough; for my part, I don't begrudge him what he wants; but I heard the people say, that no man's a gintleman who's not College-bred; and you know he's not that yet."

"You forget that he has gentle blood in his veins, Denis. There was a day when my family, the Magennises, held their heads up; and Kolumkill says that the same time is to come back agin to all the ould families. Who knows if it's altogether from himself he's takin' to the beef an' mutton, but from prophecy; he knows what he's about, I'll warrant him. For our part, it's not right for us to cross him in it; it's for the good of the church, no doubt, an' we might lose more by a blast upon the corn or the cattle, than he'd ate the other way. That's my dhrame out that I had last night about him. I thought we were all gother somewhere that I can't rightly remember; but anyhow there was a great sight of people in it, an' high doin's goin' an in the atin' way. I looked about me, an' seen ever so many priests dressed all like the Protestant clargy; our Dinis was at the head of them, wid a three-cocked hat, an' a wig upon him; he was cuttin' up beef an' mutton at the rate of a weddin', an' dhrinkin' wine in metherfuls."

"'Musha, Dinis,' says myself, 'what's all this for?'

"'Why,' says he, 'it's all for the good of the church an' the faithful. I'm now Archbishop of the county,' says he; 'the Protestants are all banished, an' we are in their place.'

"The sorra one o' myself all this time but thought he was a priest still; so says I, 'Dinny, you're a wantin' to anoint Paddy Diarmud, who's given over, an' if you don't I make haste, you won't overtake him?'

"'He must wait then till mornin',' says Dinny; 'or if he chooses to die against my will, an' the will o' the church, let him take the quensequences. Were wealthy now.'

"I was so much frightened at the kind of voice that he spoke to me in, that I awoke; an' sure enough, the first thing I heard was the fizzin' o' bacon on the pan. I wondered! who could be up so early, an' puttin' my head through the door, there was Dinny busy at it, wid an ould knife in one hand, an' an iron skiver in the other imitatin' a fork.

"'What are you doin' so early, Dinny?' says I.

"'I'm practisin',' says he.

"'What for?' says I.

"'Oh, I'm practisin',' says he, back again, 'go to bed; I'm practisin' for the church, an' the Station that's to be in Pether Rafferty's to-day.'

"Now, Dinny, between you an' me, that dhrame didn't come for nothin'. So give the gorsoon his way, an' if he chooses to be a gintleman, why let him; he'll be the more honor to thim that reared him."

"Thrue for you, indeed,—Mave; he always had a high spirit ever since he was intinded for the robes, and would have his own way and will in whatever he took into his head, right or wrong, as cleverly as if he had the authority for it."

"An' so he ought, seein' he wasn't to be slavin' at the spade, like the rest o' the family. The ways o' them that have great larnin' as he has, isn't like other people's ways—they must be humored, and have their own will, otherwise what 'ud they be betther than their neighbors?"

The other arrangements laid down by Denis, touching his determination not to be addressed so familiarly by his brothers and sisters, were next discussed in this conversation, and, of course, the same prejudice in his favor was manifested by his indulgent parents. The whole code of his injunctions was subsequently disclosed to the family in all its extent and rigor. Some of them heard it with surprise, and other with that kind of dogged indignation evinced by those who are in some degree prepared for the nature of the communication about to be laid before them. Altogether, the circumstances in which it placed them were peculiar and embarrassing. The Irish peasant can seldom bear to have the tenderness of domestic affection tampered with, whether from pride, caprice, or any other motive not related to his prejudices. In this instance the strongest feelings of the O'Shaughnessys were brunted, as it were, in hostile array against each other; and although the moral force on each side was nearly equal, still the painful revulsion produced by Denis's pride, as undervaluing their affection, and substituting the cold forms of artificial life for the warmth of honest hearts like theirs, was, in the first burst of natural fervor, strongly, and somewhat indignantly expressed.

Denis had been their pride, the privileged person among them—the individual whose talents were to throw lustre upon a nameless and unknown family; the future priest—the embryo preacher of eminence—the resistless controversialist—the holy father confessor—and, perhaps, for with that vivacity of imagination peculiar to the Irish, they could scarcely limit his exaltation—perhaps the bishop of a whole diocese. Had not the Lord Primate himself been the son of as humble a man? "And who knows," said his youngest and fairest sister, who of all the family was most devoted to him, "but Dinny might yet be a primate?" And as she spoke, the tear of affection, pride, and enthusiasm glistened in her eye. Denis, therefore, had been much, even in his youth, to their simple hearts, and far more to their hopes and expectations, than he was in all the pride of his petty polemics; but when he, before whose merits, both real and imaginary, every heart among them bowed as before the shrine of a tutelar saint, turned round, ere the destined eminence he aimed at was half attained, and laid upon their fervent affection the icy chain of pride and worldly etiquette—the act was felt keenly and unexpectedly as the acute spasm of some sudden malady. The father and mother, however, both, defended him with great warmth; and by placing his motives in that point of view which agreed best with their children's prejudices, they eventually succeeded in reconciling his brothers and sisters in some degree to the necessity of adopting the phraseology he proposed—that they might treat him with suitable respect in the eye of the world.

"It's proud of him we ought to be," said his father, "and delighted that he has sich a risin' spirit; an' sure the more respect is paid to him the greater credit he will be to ourselves."

"But, sure he has no right," said his eldest brother, "to be settin' up for a gentleman till he's priested. I'm willin' enough to sir him, only that it cuts me more than I'll say, to think that I must be callin' the boy that I'd spill the dhrop of my blood for, afther I the manner of a sthranger; and besides," he added, "I'm not clear but the neighbors will be passin' remarks upon us, as they did when you and he used to be arguin'."

"I'd like to see them that 'ud turn it into a joke," said his father; "I would let them know that Dinis O'Shaughnessy's dog is neither to be made or meddled wid in a disrespectful manner, let alone his son. We are not widout friends and connections that 'ud take our quarrel upon them in his defince, if there was a needcessity for it; but there will not, for didn't my heart lep the other day to my throat wid delight, when I saw Larry Neil put his hand to his hat to him, comin' up the Esker upon the mare; and may I never do an ill turn, if he didn't answer the bow to Larry, as if he was the priest of the parish already. It's the wondher of the world how he picks up a jinteel thing any how, an' ever did, since he was the hoith o' that."

"Why," said the mother, "what a norration yez rise about thratin' the boy as every one like him ought to be thrated. Wait till ye see him a parish priest, and then yell be comin' round him to get your daughters to keep house for him, and your sons edicated and made priests of; but now that the child takes a ginteel relish for beef and mutton, and wants to be respected, ye are mane an' low spirited enough to grumble about it."

"No mother," said his youngest sister, bursting into tears, "I'd beg it for him, sooner nor he should want; but I can't bear to be callin' my brother Dinny—sir—like a stranger. It looks as if I didn't love him, or as if he was forgettin' us, or carin' less about us nor he used to do."

This, in fact, was the root and ground of the opposition which Denis's plan received at the hands of his relations; it repressed the cordial and affectionate intercourse which had hitherto subsisted between them; but the pride of life, and, what is more, the pride of an office which ought always to be associated with humility, had got into his heart; the vanity of learning, too, thin and shallow though it was, inflated him; and the effect of both was a gradual induration of feeling—an habitual sense of his own importance, and a notion of supreme contempt for all who were more ignorant than himself.

After the first impression of pain and mortification had passed away from the minds of his brothers and sisters, it was, however, unanimously admitted that he was right; and ere long, no other feeling than one of good-humor, mingled with drollery, could be perceived among them. They were clearly convinced, that he claimed no more from strangers than was due to him; but they certainly were not prepared to hear that he had brought the exactions of personal respect so completely and unexpectedly home to themselves as he had done. The thing, too, along with being unreasonable, was awkward and embarrassing in the extreme; for there is a kind of feeling among brothers and sisters, which, though it cannot be described, is very trying to their delicacy and shamefacedness under circumstances of a similar nature. In humble life you will see a married woman who cannot call her husband after his Christian name; or a husband, who, from some extraordinary restraint, cannot address his wife, except in that distant manner which the principle I allude to dictates, and habit confirms.

Denis, however, had overcome this modesty, and felt not a whit too shamefaced to arrogate to his own learning and character the most unhesitating manifestation of their deference and respect, and they soon scrupled not to pay it.

The night of that evening was pretty far advanced, when a neighbor's son, named Condy Callaghan, came to inform the family, that Denis, when crossing the bog on his way home, had rode into a swamp, from which he found much difficulty in extricating himself, but added, "the mare is sunk to the saddle-skirts, and cannot get out widout men and ropes," In a short time a sufficient number of the neighbors were summoned together, and proceeded to the animal's relief. Denny's importance, as well as his black dress, was miserably tarnished; he stood, however, with as dignified an air as possible, and, in a bombastic style, proceeded to direct the men as to the best manner of relieving her.

"Asy, Dinny," said his brother, with a good-humored but significant smile—"larning may be very good in its place; in the mane time, lave the business in our hands rather than in your own head—or if you have e'er a scrap of Greek or Latin that 'ud charm ould Sobersides out, where was the use of sendin' for help?"

"I say," replied Dennis, highly offended, "I'll not tolerate vulgarity any longer; you must larn to address me in a more polite style. If the animal—that purblind quadruped—walked into the mire, by what logic can you produce an association between her blindness and my knowledge of Latin and Greek? But why do I degradate my own consequence by declaiming to you an eulogium upon logic? It's only throwing pearls before swine."

"I didn't mane to offind you," replied the warm-hearted brother; "I meant you no offince in what I said, so don't take it ill—we'll have Sobersides out in no time—and barrin' an extra rubbin' down to both of you, neither will be the worse, I hope."

"As to what you hope or despair, Brian, it could produce no other impression on the subtility of my fancy than pity for the man who could compare me—considering the brilliancy of my career, and the extent of my future speculations—to a quadruped like Sobersides, by asserting that I, as well as she, ought to be rubbed down! And were it not that I confront the offince with your own ignorance, I would expose you before the townland in which we stand; ay, to the whole parish—but I spare you, out of respect to my own consequence."

"I ax your pardon," said the brother, "I won't offind you in the same way again. What I said, I said to you as I thought a brother might—I ax your pardon!"

There was a slight agitation approaching to a tremor in his brother's voice, that betokened sorrow for his own impropriety in too familiarly addressing Denis, and perhaps regret that so slight and inoffensive a jest should have been so harshly received in the presence of strangers, by a brother who in reality had been his idol. He reflected upon the conversation held on that morning in the family, touching Denny's prerogative in claiming a new and more deferential deportment from them all; and he could not help feeling that there was in it a violation of some natural principle long sacred to his heart. But the all-prevading and indefinite awe felt for that sacerdotal character into which his brother was about to enter, subdued all, and reconciled him to those inroads upon violated Nature, despite her own voice, loudly expressed as it was in his bosom.

When the family was once more assembled that night, Denis addressed them in a tone, which implied that the *odium theologicum* had not prevented the contrition expressed by his brother from altogether effacing from his mind the traces of his offence.

"Unworthy of respect," he proceeded, "as it appears by some of my relations I am held," and he glanced at his brother, "yet I beg permission to state, that our worthy parochial priest, or I should rather say, the Catholic Rector of this parish, is of a somewhat different habit of thought or contemplation. I dined with him to-day—ehem—dined with him upon an excellent joint of mutton—I say, father—the mutton was good—and with his proud, pertinacious curate, whom I do not at all relish; whether, as Homer says—I enumerate his scurrilous satire, or his derogatory insinuations. His parochial pastor and spiritual superior is a gentleman, or, as Horace says, *homo factus ad unguem*—which is paraphrastically—every inch a gentleman—or more literally, a gentleman to the tops of his fingers—ehem—hem—down to the very nails—as it were.

"Well—having discussed that—*observatis observandis, quoad sacerdolem*—having passed my eulogium upon Father Finnerty—upon my word and credit though, punch is *prima facie* drink—and father, that brings me to remember an omission which I committed in my dialogue with you this morning. I forgot to say, that after my dinner, in the manner I expounded to you, it will be necessary to have a tumbler of punch—for, as Father Finnerty says, there is nothing which so effectually promotes the organs of digestion. Now, my introduction of this, in the middle of my narrative, is what the hypercritics call a Parenthesis, which certainly betrays no superficial portion of literary perusal on my part, if you could at all but understand it as well as Father Finnerty, our Worthy parochial incumbent, does. As for the curate, should I ever come to authority in the Irish hierarchy, I shall be strongly disposed to discountenance him; if it were only for his general superciliousness of conduct. So there's another clause disposed of.

"Well—to proceed—I say I have intelligence regarding myself, that will be by no means unsavory to you all. Father Finnerty and I had, about an hour before dinner this day, a long and tedious conversation, the substance of which was my future celebrity in the church. He has a claim on the Bishop, which he stated to me will be exercised in my favor, although there are several candidates for it in this parish, not one of whom, however, is within forty-five degree's of being so well qualified for college as myself. Father, is there not a jar—an *amphora*—as that celebrated satirist Juvenile has it—an *amphora*—in the chimly-brace, filled with liquor—get it, and let us *inter animosity*—I'll not be long a member of the domestic circle with you—so, upon the basis of the communication I have to make, let us, as I said, be—become sextons to animosity and care. 'Dionysius,' said Father Finnerty, addressing me, which shows, at all events, that I am not so unimportant as some of my friends would suppose—'Dionysius,' said he '*inter nos*—between you and me, I believe I have it in my power to send up a candidate to Maynooth. 'Tis true, I never make a promise—*nunquam facio votum*, except in certain cases, or, in other words, Dionysius, *exceptis excipiendis*—in which is the essence, as it were, of a proper vow.' In the meantime he proceeded—'With regard to your prospects in the church, I can only say, in the first place, and I say it with much truth and sincerity—that I'm badly off for a horse; that, however, is, as I said, *inter nos—sub sigillo*. The old garran I have is fairly worn out—and, not that I say it, your father has as pretty a colt as there is within the bounds—*intra terminos parochii mei*, within the two ends of my parish: *verbum sat*—which is, I'm sure you're a sensible and discreet young man. Your father, Dionysius, is a parishioner whom I regard and esteem to the highest degree of comparison, and you will be pleased to report my eulogium to himself and to his dacent family—and proud may they be of having so brilliant a youth among them as you are—ehem!'

"Now, you may all think that this was plain conversation; but I had read too much for that. In fact, it was logic—complate, convincing logic, every word of it. So I responded to him in what is called in the books, the *argumentum ad crumenam*; although I question but it ought to be designated here the *argumentum ad bestiam*. Said I, 'Father Finnerty, the colt, my paternal property, which you are pleased to eulogize so highly, is a good one; it was designed for myself when I should come out on the mission; however, I will undertake to say, if you get me into Maynooth, that my father, on my authority, will lend you the colt tomorrow, and the day of his claiming it will be dependent upon the fulfilment of your promise or *votum*.'

"'*Signatum et sigttlatum est*,' said he—for, indeed, the best part of the discussion was conducted in Latin; 'and now,' he continued, 'my excellent Dionysius, nothing remains but that the colt be presented—'

—"'Lent,' I responded, correcting him, 'you see, even although he was the priest—'lent,' said I; 'and your Reverence will be good enough to give the *votum* before one or two of my friends.'

"He looked at me sharply, not expecting to find such deep logic in one he conjectured to be but a tyro.

"'You will be a useful man in the church,' he added, 'and you deserve to be pushed on at all events. In the meantime, tell your father that I'll ride up and breakfast with him to-morrow, and he can have a friend or two to talk over the *compactum*.'

"So, father, there's the state of the question at present; the accomplishment of the condition is dependent upon yourself."

My readers may perceive that Denis, although a pedant, was not a fool. It has been said that no man is a hero to his *valet-de-chambre*; but I think the truth of the sentiment contained in that saying is questionable. Denis, on the contrary, was nowhere so great a man as in his own chimney-corner, surrounded by his family. It was there he was learned, accomplished, profound; next to that, he was great among those who, although not prejudiced in his favor by the bonds of affection, were too ignorant to discover those literary pranks which he played off, because he knew he could do so without detection. The basis, however, of his character was shrewd humor and good sense; and even at the stage of life which we have just described, it might have been evident to a close observer that, when a proper knowledge of his own powers, joined to a further acquaintance with the world, should enable him to cast off the boyish assumption of pedantry, a man of a keen, ready intellect and considerable penetration would remain.

Many of my readers may be inclined to exclaim that the character of Denny is not to be found in real life; but they are mistaken who think so. They are not to suppose that Denis O'Shaughnessy was the same person in his intercourse with intelligent men and scholars, that he appeared among the illiterate peasantry, or his own relations. Far from it. With the former, persons like him are awkward and bashful, or modest and unassuming, according to the bent of their natural disposition. With scholars Denis made few pretensions to superior knowledge; but, on the contrary, took refuge, if he dreaded a scrutiny into his acquirements, in the humblest acknowledgment of his limited reading, and total unacquaintance with those very topics on which he was, under other circumstances, in the habit of expatiating so fluently. In fact, were I to detail some of the scenes of his exhibitions as they were actually displayed, then I have no doubt I might be charged with coloring too highly.

When Denis had finished the oration from the chimney-corner, delivered with suitable gesticulations while he stood drying himself at the fire after the catastrophe of the swamp, a silence of some minutes followed. The promise of the colt made to the priest with such an air of authority, was a finale which the father did not expect, and by which he was not a little staggered.

"I could like it all very well," replied the father, "save an' except givin' away the coult that's worth five-an'-twenty guineas, if he's worth a *'crona-bawn*. To tell the blessed thruth, Dinis, if you had settled the business widout *that*, I'd be betther plased."

"Just exercise your contemplation upon it for a short period," replied Denis, "and you will perceive that I stipulated to lend him before witnesses; and if Father Finnerty does not matriculate me into Maynooth, then do you walk down some brilliant morning or other, and take your baste by the head, direct yourself home, hold the bridle as you proceed, and by the time you're at the rack, you'll find the horse at the manger. I have now stated the legality of the matter, and you may act as your own subtility of perception shall dictate. I have laid down the law, do you consider the equity."

"Why," said the father, "if I thought he would get you into"—

"Correct, quite correct: the cardinal point there is the if. If he does, give him the horse; but if not, reclaim the quadruped without hesitation. I am not to be kept back, if profundity and erudition can substantiate a prospect. Still, father, the easiest way is the safest, and the shortest the most expeditious."

The embarrassing situation in which the other members of the family were placed, imposed upon them a profound silence, in reference to the subject of conversation. Yet, while Denny delivered the aforesaid harangue from the chimney-corner, every eye was fixed upon him with an expression of pride and admiration which escaped not his own notice. Their deportment towards him was affectionate and respectful; but none of them could so far or so easily violate old habits as to address him according to his own wishes; they therefore avoided addressing him at all.

The next morning Father Finnerty paid them his purposed visit, and, as he had promised, arrived in time for breakfast. A few of Denis's relations were assembled, and in their presence the arrangements respecting the colt and Denny's clerical prospects were privately concluded. So far everything was tight; the time of Denny's departure for Maynooth was to be determined by the answer which Father Finnerty should receive from the bishop; for an examination must, of course, take place, which was to be conducted by the prelate, or by some other clergyman appointed for that purpose. This and the necessary preparation usual on such occasions, were the only impediments in the way of his departure for Maynooth, a place associated with so many dreams of that lowly ambition which the humble circumstances of the peasantry permit them to entertain.

The Irish people, I need scarcely observe, are a poor people; they are, also, very probably, for the same reason, an imaginative people; at all events, they are excited by occurrences which would not produce the same vivacity of emotion which they experience upon any other people in the world. This, after all, is but natural; a long endurance of hunger will render the coarsest food delicious; and, on the contrary, when the appetite is glutted with the richest viands, it requires a dish whose flavor is proportionably high and spicy to touch the jaded palate. It is so with our moral enjoyments. In Ireland, a very simple accession to their hopes or comforts produces an extraordinary elevation of mind, and so completely unlocks the sluices of their feelings, that every consideration is lost in the elation of the moment. At least it was so in Denis O'Shaughnessy's family upon this occasion.

No sooner had Father Finnerty received the colt, and pledged himself that Denny should have the place at Maynooth that was then vacant, than a tumultuous expression of delight burst from his family and relations, business was then thrown aside for the day; the house was scoured and set in order, as if it were for a festival; their best apparel was put on; every eye was bright, every heart throbbed with a delightful impulse, whilst kindness and hilarity beamed from their faces. In a short time they all separated themselves among their neighbors to communicate the agreeable tidings; and the latter, with an honest participation in their happiness, instantly laid aside their avocations, and flocked to Denis O'Shaughnessy's, that they might congratulate him and his friends upon what was considered the completion of their hopes. When the day was more advanced, several of Denny's brothers and sisters returned, and the house was nearly filled with their acquaintances and relations. Ere one o'clock had passed they wore all assembled, except old Denis, of whom, no person could give any intelligence. Talk, loud laughter, pure poteen, and good-humor, all circulated freely? the friendly neighbor unshaved, and with his Sunday coat thrown hastily over his work-day apparel, drank to Denny's health, and wished that he might "bate all Maynewth out of the face; an' sure there's no doubt of that, any how—doesn't myself remember him puttin' the explanations to Pasthorini before he was the bulk o' my fist?" His brothers and sisters now adopted with enthusiasm the terms of respect which he had prescribed for them through his father; he was Sirred and Misthered, and all but Reverenced, with a glow of affectionate triumph which they strove not to conceal. He was also overwhelmed with compliments of all hues and complexions: one reminded him of the victory he obtained over a hedge-schoolmaster who came one Sunday a distance of fifteen miles to sack him in English Grammar on the chapel-green; but as the man was no classical scholar, "Sure," observed his neighbor, "I remember well that he couldn't get a word out of Misther Denis's head there but Latin; so that the poor crathur, afther travellin' fifteen long miles, had to go home agin, the show o' the world, widout undherstandin' a sintence of the larnin' that was put an him; an' so here's wishin' you health, Misther Dinis, agra, an' no fear in life but you'll be the jewel at the prachin,' sir, plase Goodness!"

Another reminded him of "how often he proved Phaidrick Murray to be an ass, and showed him how he couldn't make out the differ atween black an' white."

"Sure, an' he did," said Phadrick, scratching his head, for he was one of the first at the house; "an' no wondher, wid his long-headed screwtations from the books. Throth, his own father was the best match, barrin' Father Lawdher that was broke of his bread, he ever met wid, till he got too many for him by the Latin an' Greek."

This allusion to old Denis occasioned his absence to be noticed.

"Can nobody tell where Denis More is?" said the wife; "my gracious, but it's quare he should be from about the place this day, any way. Brian, mavourneen, did you see him goin' any where?

"No," said Brian, "but I see him comin' down there carryin' some aitables in a basket."

Brian had scarcely ended when his father entered, bearing beef and mutton, as aforesaid, both of which he deposited upon the kitchen table, with a jerk of generosity and pride, that seemed to say, as he looked significantly at Denny— and, in fact, as he did say afterwards—"Never spare, Dinny; ate like a gintleman; make yourself as bright an' ginteel as you can; you won't want for beef an' mutton!"

Old Denis now sat down, and, after wiping the perspiration from his forehead, took the glass of poteen which the wife handed him: he held it between his finger and thumb for a moment, glanced around him upon the happy faces present, then laid it down again, fixed his eyes upon his son, and cast them once more upon the company. The affectionate father's heart was full; his breast heaved, and the large tears rolled slowly down his cheeks. By a strong effort, however, he mastered his emotion; and taking the glass again, he said in broken voice:—

"Neighbors!—God bless yez!—God bless yez!—Dinny—Dinny—I"—

The last words he pronounced with difficulty; and drinking off his glass, set it down empty upon the table. He then rose up, and shook his neighbors by the hand—

"I am," said he, "a happy man, no doubt of it, an' we're all happy; an' it's proud any father might be to hear the account of his son, that I did of mine, as I was convoyin' Father Finnerty a piece o' the way home. 'Your son,' says he, when he took that bit of a coult out o' my hand, 'will be an honor to you all. I tell you,' says he, 'that he's nearly as good a scholar, as myself, an' spakes Latin not far behind my own; an' as for a pracher,' says he, 'I can tell you that he'll be hard farther nor any man I know.' He tould me them words wid his own two lips. An' surely, neighbors," said he, relapsing into strong feeling, "you can't blame me for bein' both proud and happy of sich a son."

My readers, from the knowledge already given them of Denny's character, are probably disposed to think that his learning was thrown out on this occasion in longer words and more copious quotations than usual. This, however, was not the case; so far from that, he never displayed less pedantry, nor interspersed his conversation with fewer scraps of Latin. In fact, the proceedings of the day appeared to affect him with a tone of thought, decidedly at variance with the exuberance of joy experienced by the family. He was silent, moody, and evidently drawn by some secret reflection from the scene around him. He held a book in his hand, into which he looked from time to time, with the air of a man who balances some contingency in his mind. At length, when the conversation of those who were assembled became more loud and boisterous, he watched an opportunity of gliding out unperceived; having accomplished this, he looked cautiously about him, and finding himself not observed, he turned his steps to a glen which lay about half a mile below his father's house.

At the lowest skirt of this little valley, protected, by a few spreading hawthorns, stood a small white farm-house, more immediately shaded by a close row of elder or boor-tree, which hung over one of the gables, and covered the garden gate, together with a neat grassy seat, that was built between the gate, and the gable. It was impervious to sun and rain: one of those pretty spots which present themselves on the road-side in the country, and strike the eye with a pleasing notion of comfort; especially when, during a summer shower, the cocks and hens of the little yard are seen by the traveller who takes shelter under it, huddled up in silence, the white dust quite dry, whilst the heavy shower patters upon the leaves above, and upon the dark drenched road beside him.

Under the shade of this sat an interesting girl, aged about seventeen, named Susan Connor. She was slender, and not above the middle size; but certainly, in point of form and feature, such as might be called beautiful—handsome she unquestionably was; but be that as it may, with this rustic beauty the object of Denis's stolen visit was connected. She sat knitting under the shade of elder which we have described, a sweet picture of innocence and candor. Our hero's face, as he approached her, was certainly a fine study for any one who wished to embody the sad and the ludicrous. Desperate was the conflict between pedantry and feeling which he experienced. His manner appeared more pompous and affected than ever; yet was there blended with the flush of approaching triumph as a candidate, such woe-begone shades of distress flitting occasionally across his feature, as rendered his countenance inscrutably enigmatical.

When the usual interchange of preliminary conversation had passed, Denis took his seat beside her on the grassy bench; and after looking in several directions, and giving half a dozen hems, he thus accosted her:—

"Susan, cream of my affections, I may venture to conjecture that the fact, or *factum*, of my being the subject of *fama clamosa* today, has not yet reached your ears?"

"Now, Denis, you are at your deep larning from the books again. Can't you keep your reading for them that undherstands it, an' not be spakin' so Englified to a simple girl like me?"

"There is logic in that same, however. Do you know, Susan, I have often thought that, provided always you had resaved proper instruction, you would have made a first-rate classical scholar."

"So you tould me, Denis, the Sunday we exchanged the promise. But sure when you get me, I can larn it. Won't you tache me, Denis?"

She turned her laughing eyes archly at him as she spoke, with a look of joy and affection: it was a look, indeed, that staggered for the moment every ecclesiastical resolution within him. He returned her glance, and ran over the features of her pure and beautiful countenance for some minutes; then, placing his open hand upon his eyes, he seemed buried in reflection. At length he addressed her:—

"Susan, I am thinking of that same Sunday evening on which we exchanged the hand-promise. I say, Susan,—*dimidium animae meae*—I am in the act of meditating upon it; and sorry am I to be compel—to be under the neces—to be reduced, I say—that is redact as in the larned langua—: in other words—or terms, indeed, is more elegant—in other terms, then, Susan, I fear that what I just now alluded to, touching the *fama clamosa* which is current about me this day, will render that promise a rather premature one on both our parts. Some bachelors in my situation might be disposed to call it foolish, but I entertain a reverence—a veneration for the feelings of the feminine sex, that inclines me to use the mildest and most classical language in divulging the change that has taken place in my fortunes since I saw you last."

"What do you mane, Denis?" inquired Susan, suddenly ceasing to knit, and fixing her eyes upon him with a glance of alarm.

"To be plain, Susy, I find that Maynooth is my destination. It has been arranged between my father and Docthor Finnerty, that I must become a laborer in the vineyard; that is, that I must become a priest, and cultivate the grape. It's a sore revelation to make to an amorous maiden; but destiny will be triumphant:—

Tempora mutantur, nos et mutamur in illis."

The poor girl suddenly laid down the work on which she had been engaged, her face became the color of ashes, and the reply she was about to make died upon her lips. She again resumed her stocking, but almost instantly laid it down a second time, and appeared wholly unable either to believe or comprehend what he said.

"Denis," she at length asked, "Did you say that all is to be over between us?"

"That was my insinuation," replied Denis, "The fact is, Susy, that destiny is adverse; clean against our union in the bonds of matrimonial ecstacy. But, Susy, my charmer, I told you before that you were not destitute of logic, and I hope you will bear this heavy visitation as becomes a philosopher."

"Bear it, Denis! How ought I to bear it, after your saying and swearing, too, that neither father, nor mother, nor priest, nor anybody else would make you desart me?"

"But, Susan, my nightingale, perhaps you are not aware that there is an authority in existence to which father, mother, and all must knuckle down. That is the church, Susan. Reflect—*dulce decus meum*—that the power of the church is able to loose and unloose, to tie and untie, to forgive and to punish, to raise to the highest heaven, or to sink to the profoundest Tartarus. That power, Susan, thinks proper to claim your unworthy and enamored swain as one of the brightest Colossuses of her future glory. The Irish hierarchy is plased to look upon me as a luminary of almost superhuman brilliancy and coruscation: my talents she pronounces to be of the first magnitude; my eloquence classical and overwhelming, and my learning only adorned by that poor insignificant attribute denominated by philosophers unfathomability!—hem!—hem!"

"Denis," replied the innocent girl, "you sometimes speak that I can undherstand you; but you oftener spake in a way that I can hardly make out what you say. If it's a thing that my love for you, or the solemn promise that passed between us, would stand in your light, or prevint you from higher things as a priest, I am willing to—to—to give you up, whatever I may suffer. But you know yourself, that you brought me on from time to time undher your promise, that nothing would ever lead you to lave me in sorrow an' disappointment. Still, I say, that—But, Denis, is it thrue that you could lave me for anything?"

The innocent confidence in his truth expressed by the simplicity of her last question, staggered the young candidate; that is to say, her words, her innocence, and her affection sank deeply into his heart.

"Susan," he replied, "to tell the blessed truth, I am fairly dilemma'd. My heart is in your favor; but—but—hem—you don't know the prospect that is open to me. You don't know the sin of keeping back such a—a—a—galaxy as I am from the church. I say you don't know the sin of it. That's the difficulty. If it was a common case it would be nothing! but to keep back a person like me—a *rara avis in terris*—from the priesthood, is a sin that requires a great dale of interest with the Pope to have absolved."

"Heaven above forgive me!" exclaimed the artless girl. "In that case I wouldn't for the riches of the wide earth stand between you and. God. But I didn't know that before, Denis; and if you had tould me, I think, sooner than get into sich a sin I'd struggle to keep down my love for you, even although my heart should break."

"Poor darling," said Denis, taking her passive hand in his, "and would it go so hard with you? Break your heart! Do you love me so well as that, Susan?"

Susan's eyes turned on him for a moment, and the tears which his question drew forth gave it a full and a touching reply. She uttered not a word, but after a few deep sobs wiped her eyes, and endeavored to compose her feelings.

Denis felt the influence of her emotions; he remained silent for a short time, during which, however, ambition drew in the background all those dimly splendid visions that associate themselves with the sacerdotal functions, in a country where the people place no bounds to the spiritual power of their pastors.

"Susan," said he, after a pause, "do you know the difference between a Christian and a hathen?"

"Between a Christian an' a hathen? Why aren't hathens all sinners?"

"Very right. Faith, Susan, you would have shone at the classics. You see *dilecta cordis mei,* or, *cordi meo,* for either is good grammar—you see, Susan, the difference between a Christian and a hathen is this:— a Christian bears disappointments, with fortitude—with what is denominated Christian fortitude; whereas, on the contrary, a hathen doesn't bear disappointments at all. Now, Susan, it would cut me to the heart to find that you would become a hathen on this touching and trying occasion."

"I'll pray to God, Denis. Isn't that the way to act under afflictions?"

"Decidedly. There is no other legitimate mode of quelling a heart-ache. And, Susan, when you go to supplication you are at liberty to mention my name—no, not yet; but if I were once consecrated you might. However, it is better to sink this; say nothing about me when you pray, for, to tell you I truth, I believe you have as much influence above—*super astra*—as I have. There is one argument which I am anxious to press upon you. It is a very simple but a very respectable one after all. I am not all Ireland. You will find excellent good husbands even in this parish. There is, as the old proverb says, as good fish in the say as ever were caught. Do you catch one of them. For me, Susan, the vineyard claims me; I must, as I said, cultivate the grape. We must, consequently—hem!—we must—hem!—hem!—consequently strive to forget—hem!—I say, to forget each other. It is a trial—I know—a desperte visitation, poor fawn, upon your feelings; but, as I said, destiny will be triumphant. What is decreed, is decreed—I must go to Maynooth."

Susan rose, and her eyes flashed with an indignant sense of the cold-blooded manner in which he advised her to select another husband. She was an illiterate girl, but the purity of her feeling supplied the delicacy which reading and a knowledge of more refined society would have given her.

"Is it from your lips, Denis," she said, "that I hear sich a mane and low-minded an advice? Or do you think that with my weak, and I now see, foolish heart, settled upon you, I could turn round and fix my love upon the first that might ax me? Denis, you promised before God to be mine, and mine only; you often said and swore that you loved me above any human being; but I now see that you only intended to lead me into sin and disgrace, for indeed, and before God I don't think—I don't—I don't—believe that you ever loved me."

A burst of grief, mingled with indignation and affliction, followed the words she had uttered. Denis felt himself called on for a vindication, and he was resolved to give it.

"Susan," he returned, "your imagination is erroneous. By all the classical authors that ever were written, you are antipodialry opposed to facts. What harm is there, seeing that you and I can never be joined in wedlock—what harm is there, I say, in recommending you another husb—"

Susan would hear no more. She gathered up her stocking and ball of thread, placed them in her apron, went into her father's house, shut and bolted the door, and gave way to violent grief. All this occurred in a moment, and Denis found himself excluded.

He did not wish, however, to part from her in anger; so, after having attempted to look through the, keyhole of the door, and applied his eye in vain to the window, he at length spoke.

"Is there any body within but yourself, Susy?"

He received no reply.

"I say, Susy—*dilecta juventutis meae*—touching the recommendation—now don't be crying—touching the recommendation of another husband, by all the classics that ever were mistranslated, I meant nothing but the purest of consolation. If I did, may I be reduced to primeval and aboriginal ignorance! But you know yourself, that they never prospered who prevented a *rara avis* like me from entering the church—from laboring in the vineyard, and cultivating the grape. Don't be hathenish; but act with a philosophy suitable to so dignified an occasion—Farewell! *Macte virtute*, and be firm. I swear again by all the class—"

The appearance of a neighbor caused him to cut short his oath. Seeing that the man approached the house, he drew off, and returned home, more seriously affected by Susan's agitation than he was willing to admit even to himself.

This triumph over his affection was, in fact, only the conquest of one passion over another. His attachment to Susan Connor was certainly sincere, and ere the prospects of his entering Maynooth were unexpectedly brought near him, by the interference of Father Finnerty, his secret purpose all along had been to enter with her into the state of matrimony, rather than into the church. Ambition, however, is beyond all comparison the most powerful principle of human conduct, and so Denny found it. Although his unceremonious abandonment of Susan appeared heartless and cruel, yet it was not effected on his part without profound sorrow and remorse. The two principles, when they began to struggle in his heart for supremacy, resembled the rival destinies of Caesar and Mark Antony. Love declined in the presence of ambition; and this, in proportion as all the circumstances calculated to work upon the strong imagination of a young man naturally fond of power, began to assume an appearance of reality. To be, in the course of a few years, a *bona fide* priest; to possess unlimited sway over the fears and principles of the people; to be endowed with spiritual gifts to he knew not what extent; and to enjoy himself as he had an opportunity of seeing Father Finnerty and his curate do, in the full swing of convivial pleasure, upon the ample hospitality of those who, in addition to this, were ready to kiss the latchet of his shoes—were, it must be admitted, no inconsiderable motives in influencing the conduct of a person reared in an humble condition of life. The claims of poor Susan, her modesty, her attachment, and her beauty—were all insufficient to prevail against such a host of opposing motives; and the consequence, though bitter, and subversive of her happiness, was a final determination on the part of Denny, to acquaint her, with a kind of *ex-officio* formality, that all intercourse upon the subject of their mutual attachment must cease between them. Notwithstanding his boasted knowledge, however, he was ignorant of sentiment, and accordingly confined himself, as I have intimated, to a double species of argument; that is to say, first, the danger and sin of opposing the wishes of the church which had claimed him, as he said, to labor in the vineyard; and secondly, the undoubted fact, that there were plenty of good husbands besides himself in the world, from some one of which, he informed her, he had no doubt, she could be accommodated.

In the meantime, her image, meek, and fair, and uncomplaining, would from time to time glide into his imagination; and the melody of her voice send its music once more to his vaccillating heart. He usually paused then, and almost considered himself under the influence of a dream; but ambition, with its train of shadowy honors, would immediately present itself, and Susan was again forgotten.

When he rejoined the company, to whom he had given the slip, he found them all gone, except about six or eight whom his father had compelled to stop for dinner. His mind was now much lighter than it had been before his interview with Susan, nor were his spirits at all depressed by perceiving that a new knife and fork lay glittering upon the dresser for his own particular use.

"Why, thin, where have you been all this time," said the father, "an' we wantin' to know whether you'd like the mutton to be boiled or roasted!"

"I was soliloquizing in the glen below," replied Denny, once more assuming his pedantry, "meditating upon the transparency of all human events; but as for the beef and mutton, I advise you to boil the beef, and roast the mutton, or vice versa, to boil the mutton, and roast the beef. But I persave my mother has anticipated me, and boiled them both with that flitch of bacon that's playing the vagrant in the big pot there. *Tria juncla in uno*, as Horace says in the Epodes, when expatiating upon the Roman Emperors—ehem!"

"Misther Denis," said one of those present, "maybe you'd tell us upon the watch, what the hour is, if you plase, sir; myself never can know right at all, except by the shadow of the sun from the corner of our own gavel."

"Why," replied Denis, pulling it out with much pomp of manner, "it's just half-past two to a quarter of a minute, and a few seconds."

"Why thin what a quare thing entirely a watch is," the other continued; "now what makes you hould it to your ear, Misther Denis, if you plase?"

"The efficient cause of that, Larry, is, that the drum of the ear, you persave—the drum of the ear—is enabled to catch the intonations produced by the machinery of its internal operations—otherwise the fact of applying it to the ear would be unnecessary—altogether unnecessary."

"Dear me! see what it is to have the knowledge, any way! But isn't it quare how it moves of itself like a livin' crathur? How is that, Misther Denis?"

"Why, Larry,—ehem—you see the motions of it are—that is—the works or operations, are all continually going; and sure it is from that explanation that we say a watch goes well. That's more than you ever knew before, Larry."

"Indeed it surely is, sir, an' is much oblaged to you, Misther Denis; sure if I ever come to wear a watch in my fob, I'll know something about it, anyhow."

For the remainder of that day Denis was as learned and consequential as ever; his friends, when their hearts were opened by his father's hospitality, all promised him substantial aid in money, and in presents of such articles as they supposed might be serviceable to him in Maynooth. Denny received their proffers of support with suitable dignity and gratitude. A scene of bustle and preparation now commenced among them, nor was Denny himself the least engaged; for it somehow happened, that notwithstanding his profound erudition, he felt it necessary to read night or day in order to pass with more eclat the examination which he had to stand before the bishop ere his appointment to Maynooth. This ordeal was to occur upon a day fixed for the purpose, in the ensuing month; and indeed Denis occupied as much of the intervening period in study as his circumstances would permit. His situation was, at this crisis, certainly peculiar. Every person related to him in the slightest degree contrived to revive their relationship; his former school-fellows, on hearing that he was actually destined to be of the church, renewed their acquaintance with him, and those who had been servants to his father, took the liberty of speaking to him upon the strength of that fact. No child, to the remotest shade of affinity, was born, for which he did not stand godfather; nieces and nephews thickened about him, all with remarkable talents, and many of them, particularly of the nieces, said to be exceedingly genteel—very thrifty for their ages, and likely to make excellent housekeepers. A strong likeness to himself was also pointed out in the features of his nephews, one of whom had his born nose—another his eyes—and a third again had his brave high-flown way with him. In short, he began to feel some of the inconveniences of greatness; and, like it, to be surrounded by cringing servility and meanness. When he went to the chapel he was beset, and followed from place to place, by a retinue of friends who were all anxious to secure to themselves the most conspicuous marks of his notice. It was the same thing in fair or market; they contended with each other who should do him most honor, or afford to him and his father's immediate family the most costly treat, accompanied by the grossest expressions of flattery. Every male infant born among them was called Dionysius; and every female one Susan, after his favorite sister. All this, to a lad like Denis, already remarkable for his vanity, was very trying; or rather, it absolutely turned his brain, and made him probably as finished a specimen of pride, self-conceit, and domineering arrogance, mingled with a kind of lurking humorous contempt for his cringing relations, as could be displayed in the person of some shallow but knavish prime minister, surrounded by his selfish sycophants, whom he encourages and despises.

At home he was idolized—overwhelmed with respect and deference. The slightest intimation of his wish was a command to them; the beef, and fowl, and mutton, were at hand in all the variety of culinary skill, and not a soul in the house durst lay a hand upon his knife and fork but himself. In the morning, when the family were to be seen around the kitchen table at their plain but substantial breakfast, Denis was lording it in solitary greatness over an excellent breakfast of tea and eggs in another room.

It was now, too, that the king's English, as well as the mutton, was carved and hacked to some purpose; epithets prodigiously long and foreign to the purpose were pressed into his conversation, for no other reason than because those to whom he spoke could not understand them; but the principal portion of his time was devoted to study. The bishop, he had heard, was a sound scholar, and exceedingly scrupulous in recommending any to Maynooth, except such as were well versed in the preparatory course. Independently of this, he was anxious, he said, to distinguish himself in his examination, and, if possible, to sustain as high a character with the bishop and his fellow-students, as he did among the peasantry of his own neighborhood.

At length the day approached. The bishop's residence was not distant more than a few hours' ride, and he would have sufficient time to arrive there, pass his examination, and return in time for dinner. On the eve of his departure, old

Denis invited Father Finnerty, his curate and about a dozen relations and friends, to dine with him the next day; when—Denis having surmounted the last obstacle to the accomplishment of his hopes—their hearts could open without a single reflection to check the exuberance of their pride, hospitality, and happiness.

I have often said to my friends, and I now repeat it in print, that after all there is no people bound up so strongly to each other by the ties of domestic life as the Irish. On the night which preceded this joyous and important day, a spirit of silent but tender affection dwelt in every heart of the O'Shaughnessys. The great point of interest was Denis. He himself was serious, and evidently labored under that strong anxiety so natural to a youth in his circumstances. A Roman Catholic bishop, too, is a personage looked upon by the people with a kind of feeling that embodies in it awe, reverence, and fear. Though, in this country, an humble man possessing neither the rank in society, outward splendor, nor the gorgeous profusion of wealth and pomp which characterize a prelate of the Established Church; yet it is unquestionable that the gloomy dread, and sense of formidable power with which they impress the minds of the submissive peasantry, immeasurably surpass the more legitimate influence which any Protestant dignitary could exercise over those who stand, with respect to him, in a more rational and independent position.

It was not surprising that Denis, who practised upon ignorant people that petty despotism for which he was so remarkable, should now, on coming in contact with great spiritual authority, adopt his own principles, and relapse from the proud pedant into the cowardly slave. True it is that he presented a most melancholy specimen of independence in a crisis where moral courage was so necessary; but his dread of the coming day was judiciously locked up in his own bosom. His silence and apprehension were imputed to the workings of a mind learnedly engaged in arranging the vast stores of knowledge with which it was so abundantly stocked; his moody picture of the bishop's brow; his reflection that he was going before so sacred a person, as a candidate for the church, with his heart yet redolent of earthly affection for Susan Connor; his apprehension that the bishop's spiritual scent might sagaciously smell it out, were all put down by the family to the credit of uncommon learning, which, as his mother observed truly, "often makes men do quare things." His embarrassments, however, inasmuch as they were ascribed by them to wrong causes, endeared him more to their hearts than ever. Because he spoke little, neither the usual noise nor bustle of a large family disturbed the silence of the house; every word was uttered that evening in a low tone, at once expressive of tenderness and respect. The family supper was tea, in compliment to Denis; and they all partook of it with him. Nothing humbles the mind, and gives the natural feelings their full play, so well as a struggle in life, or the appearance of its approach.

"Denis," said the father, "the time will come when we won't have you at all among us; but, thank goodness, you'll be in a bettther place."

Denis heard him not, and consequently made no reply.

"They say Maynewth's a tryin' place, too," he continued, "an' I'd be sorry to see him pulled down to anatomy, like some of the scarecrows that come qut of it. I hope you'll bear it betther."

"Do you speak to me?" said Denis, awaking out of a reverie.

"I do, sir," replied the father; and as he uttered the words the son perceived that his eyes were fixed upon him with an expression of affectionate sorrow and pride.

The youth was then in a serious mood, free from all the dominion of that learned mania under which he had so frequently signalized himself: the sorrow of his father, and a consciousness of the deep affection and unceasing kindness which he had ever experienced from him, joined to a recollection of their former friendly disputes and companionship, touched Denny to the quick. But the humility with which he applied to him the epithet sir, touched him most. What! thought he—ought my affectionate father to be thrown to such a distance from a son, who owes everything to his love and goodness! The thought of his stooping so humbly before him smote the boy's heart, and the tears glistened in his eyes.

"Father," said he, "you have been kind and good to me, beyond my deserts; surely then I cannot bear to hear you address me in that manner, as if we were both strangers. Nor while I am with you, shall any of you so address me. Remember that I am still your son and their brother."

The natural affection displayed in this speech soon melted the whole family into tears—not excepting Denis himself, who felt that grief which we experience when about to be separated for the first time from those we love.

"Come over, avourneen," said his mother, drying her eyes with the corner of her check apron: "come over, *acushla machree*, an' sit beside me: sure although we're sorry for you, Denis, it's proud our hearts are of you, an' good right we have, a sullish! Come over, an let me be near you as long as I can, any way."

Denis placed himself beside her, and the proud mother drew his head over upon her bosom, and bedewed his face with a gush of tears.

"They say," she observed, "that it's sinful to shed tears when there's no occasion for grief; but I hope it's no sin to cry when one's heart is full of somethin' that brings them to one's eyes, whether they will or not."

"Mave," said the father, "I'll miss him more nor any of you: but sure he'll often send letters to us from Maynewth, to tell us now he's gettin' on; an' we'll be proud enough, never fear."

"You'll miss me, Denis," said his favorite sister, who was also called Susan; "for you'll find no one in Maynewth that will keep your linen so white as I did: but never fear, I'll be always knittin' you stockings; an' every year I'll make you half-a-dozen shirts, and you'll think them more natural nor other shirts, when you know they came from your own home—from them that you love! Won't you, Denis?"

"I will, Susy; and I will love the shirts for the sake of the hands that made them."

"And I won't allow Susy Connor to help me as she used to do: they'll be all Alley's sewin' and mine."

"The poor colleen—listen to her!" exclaimed the affectionate father; "indeed you will, Susy; ay, and hem his cravats, that we'll send him ready made an' all."

"Yes," replied Denis, "but as to Susy Connor—hem—why, upon considera—he—hem—upon second thoughts, I don't see why you should prevent her from helping you; she's a neighbor's daughter, and a well-wisher, of whose prosperity in life I'd always wish to hear.

"The poor girl's very bad in her health, for the last three weeks," observed his other sister Alley: "she has lost her appetite, an' is cast down entirely in her spirits. You ought to go an' see her, Denis, before you set out for the college, if it was only on her dacent father's account. When I was tellin' her yesterday that you wor to get the bishop's letter for Maynewth to-morrow, she was in so poor a state of health that she nearly fainted. I had to give her a drink of wather, and sprinkle her face with it. Well, she's a purty crathur, an' a good girl, an' was always that, dear knows!"

"Denis achree," said his mother, somewhat alarmed, "are you any way unwell? Why your heart's batin' like a new catched chicken! Are you sick, acushla; or are you used to this?"

"It won't signify," replied Denis, gently raising himself from his mother's arms, "I will sit up, mother; it's but a sudden stroke or two of *tremor cordis*, produced probably by having my mind too much upon one object."

"I think," said his father, "he will be the betther of a little drop of the poteen made into punch, an' for that matter we can all take a sup of it; as there's no one here but ourselves, we will have it snug an' comfortable."

Nothing resembles an April day more than the general disposition of the Irish people. When old Denis's proposal for the punch was made, the gloom which hung over the family—originating, as it did, more in joy than in soitow—soon began to disappear. Their countenances gradually brightened, by and by mirth stole out, and ere the punch had accomplished its first round, laughter, and jest, and good-humor,—each, in consequence of the occasion, more buoyant and vivacious than usual, were in full play. Denis himself, when animated by the unexcised liquor, threw off his dejection, and' ere the night was half spent found himself in the highest region of pedantry.

"I would not," said he, "turn my back upon any other candidate in the province, in point of preparatory excellence and ardency of imagination. I say, sitting here beside you, my worthy and logical father, I would not retrograde from any candidate for the honors of the Catholic Church in the province—in the kingdom—in Europe; and it is not improbable but I might progradiate another step, and say Christendom at large. And now, what's a candidate? Father, you have some apprehension in you, and are a passable second-hand controversialist—what's a candidate? Will you tell me?"

"I give it up, Denis; but you'll tell us."

"Yes, I will tell you. Candidate signifies a man dressed in fustian; it comes from *candidus*, which is partly Greek, partly Latin, and partly Hebrew. It was the learned designation for Irish linen, too, which in the time of the Romans was in great request at Home; but it was changed to signify fustian, because it was found that everything a man promised on becoming a candidate for any office, turned out to be only fustian when he got it."

"Denis, avourneen," said his mother, "the greatest comfort myself has is to be thinkin' that when you're a priest, you can be sayin' masses for my poor sinful sowl."

"Yes, there is undoubtedly comfort in, that reflection; and depend upon it, my dear mother, that I'll be sure to clinch your masses in the surest mode. I'll not fly over them like Camilla across a field of potato oats, without discommoding a single walk, as too many of my worthy brethren—I mane as! too many of those whose worthy brother I will soon be—do in this present year of grace. I'm no fool at the Latin, but, as I'm an unworthy candidate for Maynooth, I cannot even understand every fifteenth word they say when reading mass, independently of the utter scorn with which they treat; these two Scholastic old worthies, called! Syntax and Prosody."

"Denis," said the father, "nothing would give me greater delight than to be present at your first mass, an' your first sarmon; and next to that I would like to be stumpin' about wid a dacent staff in my hand, maybe wid a bit of silver on the head of it, takin' care of your place when you'd have a parish."

"At all events, if you're not with me, father, I'll keep you comfortable wherever you'll be, whether in this world or the other; for, plase goodness, I'll have some influence in both.—When I get a parish, however, it is not improbable that I may have occasion to see company; the neighboring gentlemen will be apt to relish my society, particularly those who are addicted to conviviality; and our object will be to render ourselves as populous as possible; now, whether in that case it would be compatible—but never fear, father, whilst I have the means, you or one of the family shall never want."

"Will you let the people be far behind in their dues, Denis?" inquired Brian.

"No, no—leave that point to my management. Depend upon it, I'll have them like mice before me—ready to run into the first augerhole they meet. I'll collect lots of oats, and get as much yarn every year as would clothe three regiments of militia, or, for that matter, of dragoons. I'll appoint my stations, too, in the snuggest farmers' houses in the parish, just as Father Finnerty, our worthy parochial priest, ingeniously contrives to do. And, to revert secondarily to the collection of the oats, I'll talk liberally to the Protestant boddaghs; give the Presbyterians a learned homily upon civil and religious freedom: make hard hits with them at that Incubus, the Established Church; and, never fear, but I shall fill bag after bag with good corn from many of both creeds."

"That," said Brian, "will be givin' them the bag to hould in airnest."

"No, Brian, but it will be makin' them fill the bag when I hold it, which will be better still."

"But," said Susan, "who'll keep house for you? You know that a priest can't live widout a housekeeper."

"That, Susy," replied Denis, "is, and will be the most difficult point on which to accomplish anything like a satisfactory determination. I have nieces enough, however. There's Peter Finnegan's eldest daughter Mary, and Hugh Tracy's Ailsey—(to whom he added about a dozen and a half more)—together with several yet to be endowed with existence, all of whom will be brisk candidates for the situation."

"I don't think," replied Mrs. O'Shaughnessy, "that you'll ever get any one who'd be more comfortable about you nor your own ould mother. What do you think of takin' myself, Denis?"

"Ay, but consider the accomplishments in the culinary art—*in re vel in arte culinaria*—which will be necessary for my housekeeper to know. How would you, for instance, dress a dinner for the bishop if he happened to pay me a visit, as you may be certain he will? How would you make pies and puddings, and disport your fancy through all the varieties of roast and boil? How would you dress a fowl that it would stand upon a dish as if it was going to dance a hornpipe? How would you amalgamate the different genera of wine with boiling fluid and crystallized saccharine matter? How would you dispose of the various dishes upon the table according to high life and mathematics? Wouldn't you be too old to bathe my feet when I'd be unwell? Wouldn't you be too old to bring me my whey in the morning soon as I'd awake, perhaps with a severe headache, after the plenary indulgence of a clerical compotation? Wouldn't you be too old to sit up till the middle of the nocturnal hour, awaiting my arrival home? Wouldn't you be—"

"Hut, tut, that's enough, Denny, I'd never do at all. No, no, but I'll sit a clane, dacent ould woman in the corner upon a chair that you'll get made for me. There I'll be wid my pipe and tobacco, smokin' at my aise, chattin' to the sarvints, and sometimes discoorsin' the neighbors that'll come to inquire for you, when they'll be sittin' in the kitchen waitin' till you get through your office. Jist let me have that, Dinny achora, and I'll be as happy as the day's long."

"And I on the other side," said his father, naturally enough struck with the happy simplicity of the picture which his wife drew, "on the other side, Mave, a snug, dacent ould man, chattin' to you across the fire, proud to see the bishop an' the gintlemen about him. An' I wouldn't ax to be taken into the parlor at all, except, maybe, when there would be nobody there but yourself, Denis; an' that your mother an' I would go into the parlor to get a glass of punch, or, if it could be spared, a little taste of wine for novelty."

"And so you shall, both of you—you, father, at one side of the hob, and my mother here at the other, the king and queen of my culinarian dominions. But practice taciturnity a little—I'm visited by the muse, and must indulge in a strain of vocal melody—hem—'tis a few lines of my own composure, the offspring of a moment of inspiration by the nine female Heliconians; but before I incipiate, here's to my own celebrity to-morrow, and afterwards all your healths!"

He then proceeded to sing in his best style a song composed, as he said, by himself, but which, as the composition was rather an eccentric one, we decline giving.

"Denis," said his brother, "you'll have great sport at the Station's."

"Yes, Brian, most inimitable specimen of fraternity, I do look into the futurity of a station with great complacency. Hem—in the morning I rise up in imagination, and after reading part of my office, I and my curate—*ego et coadjutor metis*—or, if I get a large parish, perhaps I and my two curates—*ego et coudjutores mei*—order our horses, and of a fine, calm summer morning we mount them as gracefully as three throopers. The sun is up, and of coorse the moon is down, and the glitter of the light, the sparkling of the dew, the canticles of the birds, and the *melodiotis* cowing of the crows in Squire Grimshaw's rookery—"

"Why, Denis, is it this parish you'll have?"

"Silence, silence, till I complate my rural ideas—in some gentleman's rookery at all events; the thrush here, the blackbird there, the corn-craik chanting its varied note in another place, and so on. In the meantime we reverend sentimentalists advance, gazing with odoriferous admiration upon the prospect about us, and expatiating in the purest of Latin upon the beauties of unsophisticated nature. When we meet the peasants going out to their work, they put their hands to their hats for us; but as I am known to be the parochial priest, it is to me the salutation is directed, which I return with the air of a man who thinks nothing of such things; but, I on the contrary, knows them to be his due. The poor creatures of curates you must know, don't presume to speak of themselves, but simply answer whenever I condescend to propose conversation, for I'll keep them down, never fear. In this edifying style we proceed—I a few steps in advance, and they at a respectful distance behind me, the heads of their horses just to my saddle skirts—my clerical boots as brilliant as the countenance of Phoebus, when decked with rosy smiles, theirs more subordinately polished, for there should be gradations in all things, and humility is the first of virtues in a Christian curate. My bunch of gold sales stands out proudly from my anterior rotundity, for by this time, plase God, I'll be getting frolicsome and corpulent: they with only a poor bit of ribbon, and a single two-penny kay, stained with verdigrace. In the meantime, we come within sight of the wealthy farmer's house, wherein we are to hold the edifying solemnity of a station. There is a joyful appearance of study and bustle about the premises: the peasantry are flocking towards it, dressed in their best clothes; the proprietors of the mansion itself are running out to try if we are in appearance, and the very smoke disports itself hilariously in the air, and bounds up as if it was striving to catch the first glimpse of the clargy. When we approach, the good man—*pater-familias*—comes out to meet us, and the good woman—*mater-farmilias*—comes curtseying from the door to give the head *milliafailtha*. No sooner do we parsave ourselves noticed, then out comes the Breviary, and in a moment we are at our morning devotions. I being the rector, am particularly grave and dignified. I do not speak much, but am rather sharp, and order the curates, whom I treat, however, with great respect before the people, instantly to work. This impresses those who are present with awe and reverence for us all, especially for Father O'Shaughnessy himself—(that's me).—I then take a short turn or two across the floor, silently perusing my office, after which I lay it aside, and relax into a little conversation with the people of the house, to show that I can conciliate by love as readily as I can impress them with fear; for, you see *divide et impera* is as aptly applied to the passions as to maxims of state policy—ehem. I then go to my tribunal, and first hear the man and woman and family of the house, and afther them the other penitents according as they can come to me.

"Thus we go on absolving in great style, till it is time for the *matutinal* meal—vulgarly called breakfast; when the whiskey, eggs, toast, and tea as strong as Hercules, with ham, fowl, beef-steaks, or mutton-chops, all pour in upon us in the full tide of hospitality. Helter-skelter, cut and thrust, right and left, we work away, till the appetite reposes itself upon the cushion of repletion: and off we go once more, full an' warm, to the delicate employment of adjudicating upon sin and transgression, until dinner comes, when, having despatched as many as possible—for the quicker we get through them the better—we set about despatching what is always worth a ship-load of such riff-raff—*videlicet*, a good and extensive dinner. Oh, ye pagan gods of eating and drinking, Bacchus and—let me see who the presiding deity of good feeding was in the Olympian synod—as I'm an unworthy candidate I forget that topic of learning; but no matter, *non constat*. Oh, ye pagan professors of ating and drinking, Bacchus, and Epicurus, and St. Heliogabalus, Anthony of Padua, and Paul the Hermit, who poached for his own venison, St. Tuck, and St. Takem, St. Drinkem, and St. Eatem, with all the other reverend worthies, who bore the blushing honors of the table thick upon your noses, come and inspire your unworthy candidate, while he essays to chant the praises of a Station dinner!

"Then, then, does the priest appropriate to himself his due share of enjoyment Then does he, like Elias, throw his garment of inspiration upon his coadjutors. Then is the goose cut up, and the farmer's distilled Latin is found to be purer and more edifying than the distillation of Maynooth.

'Drink deep, or taste not that Pierian spring, A little learning here's a dangerous thing.'

And so it is, as far as this inspiring language is concerned. A station dinner is the very pinnacle of a priest's happiness. There is the fun and frolic; then does the lemon-juice of mirth and humor come out of their reverences, like secret writing, as soon as they get properly warm. The song and the joke, the laugh and the leer, the shaking of hands, the making of matches, and the projection of weddings,—och, I must conclude, or my brisk fancy will dissolve in the deluding vision! Here's to my celebrity to-morrow, and may the Bishop catch a Tartar in your son, my excellent and logical father!—as I tell you among ourselves he will do. Mark me, I say it, but it's *inter nos*, it won't go further; but should he trouble me with profundity, may be I'll make a *ludibrium* of him."

"But you forget the weddings and christenings, Denis; you'll have great sport at them too."

"I can't remember three things at a time, Brian; but you are mistaken, however, I had them snug in one corner of my cranium. The weddings and the christenings! do you think I'll have nothing to do in them, you! *stultus* you?"

"But, Denis, is there any harm in the priests enjoying themselves, and they so holy as we know they are?" inquired his mother.

"Not the least in life; considering what severe fasting, and great praying they have; besides it's necessary for them to take something to put the sins of the people out of their heads, and that's one reason why they are often jolly at Stations."

"My goodness, what light Denis can throw upon anything!"

"Not without deep study, mother; but let us have another portion of punch each, afther which I'll read a Latin De Profundis, and we'll go to bed, I must be up early tomorrow; and, Brian, you'll please to have the black mare saddled and my spur brightened as jinteely as you can, for I must go in as much state and grandeur as possible." Accordingly, in due time, after hearing the De Profundis, which Denis read in as sonorous a tone, and as pompous a manner, as he could assume, they went to bed for the night, to dream of future dignities for their relative.

When Denis appeared the next morning, it was evident that the spirit of prophecy in which he had contemplated the enjoyments annexed to his ideal station on the preceding night, had departed from him. He was pale and anxious, as in the early part of the previous evening. At breakfast, his very appetite treacherously abandoned him, despite the buttered toast and eggs which his mother forced upon him with such tender assiduity, in order, she said, to make him stout against the Bishop. Her solicitations, however, were vain; after attempting to eat to no purpose, he arose and began to prepare himself for his journey. This, indeed, was a work of considerable importance, for, as they had no looking-glass, he was obliged to dress himself over a tub of water, in which, since truth must be told, he saw a very cowardly visage. In due time, however, he was ready to proceed upon his journey, apparelled in a new suit of black that sat stiffly and awkwardly upon him, crumpled in a manner that enabled any person, at a glance, to perceive that it was worn for the first time. When he was setting out, his father approached him with a small jug of holy water in his hand. "Denis," said he, "I think you won't be the worse for a sprinkle of this;" and he accordingly was about to shake it with a little brush over his person, when Denis arrested his hand.

"Easy, father," he replied, "you don't remember that my new clothes are on. I'll just take a little with, my fingers, for you know one drop is as good as a thousand."

"I know that," said the father, "but on the other hand you know it's not lucky to refuse it."

"I didn't refuse it," rejoined Denis, "I surely took a quantum suff. of it with my own hand."

"It was very near a refusal," said the father, in a disappointed and somewhat sorrowful tone; "but it can't be helped now. I'm only sorry you put it and quantum suff. in connection at all. Quantum suff. is what Father Finnerty says, when he will take no more punch; and it doesn't argue respect in you to make as little of a jug of holy wather as he does of a jug of punch."

"I'm sarry for it too," replied Denis, who was every whit as superstitious as his father; "and to atone for my error, I desire you will sprinkle me all over with it—clothes and all."

The father complied with this, and Denis was setting out, when his mother exclaimed, "Blessed be them above us, Denis More! Look at the boy's legs! There's luck! Why one of his stockin's has the wrong side out, and it's upon the right leg too! Well, this will be a fortunate day for you, Denis, any way; the same thing never happened myself, but something good followed it."

This produced a slight conflict between Denis's personal vanity and superstition; but on this occasion superstition prevailed: he even felt his spirits considerably elevated by the incident, mounted the mare, and after jerking himself once or twice in the saddle, to be certain that all was right, he touched her with the spur, and set out to be examined by the Bishop, exclaiming as he went, "Let his lordship take care that I don't make a *ludibrium* of him."

The family at that moment all came to the door, where they stood looking after, and admiring him, until he turned a corner of the road, and left their sight.

Many were the speculations entered into during his absence, as to the fact, whether or not he would put down the bishop in the course of the examination; some of them holding that he could do so if he wished; but others of them denying that it was possible for him, inasmuch as he had never received holy orders.

The day passed, but not in the usual way, in Denis More O'Shaughnessy's. The females of the family were busily engaged in preparing for the dinner, to which Father Finnerty, his curate, and several of their nearest and wealthiest friends had been invited; and the men in clearing out the stables and other offices for the horses of the guests. Pride and satisfaction were visible on every face, and that disposition to cordiality and to the oblivion of everything unpleasant to the mind, marked, in a prominent manner, their conduct and conversation. Old Denis went, and voluntarily spoke to a neighbor, with whom he had not exchanged a word, except in anger, for some time. He found him at work in the field, and, advancing with open hand and heart, he begged his pardon for any offence he might have given him.

"My son," said he, "is goin' to Maynooth; and as he is a boy that we have a good right to be proud of, and as our friends are comin' to ate their dinner wid us to-day, and as—as my heart is to full to bear ill-will against any livin' sowl, let alone a man that I know to be sound at the heart, in spite of all that has come between us—I say, Darby, I forgive you, and I expect pardon for my share of the offence. There's the hand of an honest man—let us be as neighbors ought to be, and not divided into parties and factions against one another, as we have been too long. Take your dinner wid us to-day, and let us hear no more about ill-will and unkindness."

"Denis," said his friend, "it ill becomes you to spake first. 'Tis I that ought to do that, and to do it long ago too; but you see, somehow, so long as it was to be decided by blows between the families, I'd never give in. Not but that I might do so, but my sons, Denis, wouldn't hear of it. Throth, I'm glad of this, and so will they too; for only for the honor and glory of houldin' out, we might be all friends through other long ago. And I'll tell you what, we couldn't do better, the two factions of us, nor join and thrash them Haigneys that always put between us."

"No, Darby, I tell you, I bear no ill-will, no bad thoughts agin any born Christian this day, and I won't hear of that. Come to us about five o'clock: we're to have Father Finnerty, and Father Molony, his curate: all friends, man, all friends; and Denny, God guard him this day, will be home, afther passin' the Bishop, about four o'clock."

"I always thought that gorsoon would come to somethin'. Why it was wondherful how he used to discoorse upon the chapel-green, yourself and himself: but he soon left you behind. And how he sealed up poor ould Dixon, the parish dark's mouth, at Barny Boccagh's wake. God rest his soul! It was talkin' about the Protestant church they wor. 'Why,' said Misther Denis, 'you ould termagent, can you tell me who first discovered your church?' The dotin' ould crathur began of hummin', and hawin', and advisin' the boy to have more sense. 'Come,' said he, 'you ould canticle, can you answer? But for fear you can't, I'll answer for you. It was the divil discovered it, one fine mornin' that he went out to get an appetite, bein' in delicate health.' Why, Denis, you'd tie all that wor present wid a rotten sthraw."

"Darby, I ax your pardon over agin for what came between us; and I see now betther than I did, that the fault of it was more mine nor yours. You'll be down surely about five o'clock?"

"I must go and take this beard off o' me, and clane myself; and I may as well do that now: but I'll be down, never fear."

"In throth the boy was always bright!—ha, ha, ha!—and he sobered Dixon?"

"Had him like a judge in no time."

"Oh, he would do it—he could do that, at all times. God be wid you, Darby, till I see you in the evenin'."

"*Bannaght lhath*, Denis, an' I'm proud we're as we ought to be."

About four o'clock, the expected guests began to assemble at Denis's; and about the same hour one might perceive Susan O'Shaughnessy running out to a stile a little above the house, where she stood for a few minutes, with her hand shadingher eyes, looking long and intensely towards the direction from which she expected her brother to return. Hitherto, however, he could not be discovered in the distance, although scarcely five minutes elapsed during the intervals of her appearance at the stile to watch him. Some horsemen she did notice; but after straining her eyes eagerly and anxiously, she was enabled only to report, with a dejected air, that they were their own friends coming from a distant part of the parish, to be present at the dinner. At length, after a long and eager look, she ran in with an exclamation of delight, saying—

"Thank goodness, he's comin' at last; I see somebody dressed in black ridin' down the upper end of Tim Marly's boreen, an' I'm sure an' certain it must be Denis, from his dress!"

"I'll warrant it is, my colleen," replied her father; "he said he'd be here before the dinner would be ready, an' it's widin a good hour of that. I'll thry myself."

He and his daughter once more went out; but, alas! only to experience a fresh disappointment. Instead of Denis, it was Father Finnerty; who, it appeared, felt as anxious to be in time for dinner, as the young candidate himself could have done. He was advancing at a brisk trot, not upon the colt which had been presented to him, but upon his old nag, which seemed to feel as eager to get at Denis's oats, as its owner did to taste his mutton.

"I see, Susy, we'll have a day of it, plase goodness," observed Denis to the girl; "here's Father Finnerty, and I wouldn't for more nor I'll mention that he had staid away: and I hope the coidjuther will come as well as himself. Do you go in, aroon, and tell them he's comin', and I'll go and meet him."

Most of Denis's friends were now assembled, dressed in their best apparel, and Raised to the highest pitch of good humor; no man who knows the relish with which Irishmen enter into convivial enjoyments, can be ignorant of the remarkable flow of spirits which the prospect of an abundant and hospitable dinner produces among them.

Father Finnerty was one of those priests who constitute a numerous species in Ireland; regular, but loose and careless in the observances of his church, he could not be taxed with any positive neglect of pastoral duty. He held his stations at stated times and places, with great exactness, but when the severer duties annexed to them were performed, he relaxed into the boon companion, sang his song, told his story, laughed his laugh, and occasionally danced his dance, the very *beau ideal* of a rough, shrewd, humorous divine, who, amidst the hilarity of convivial mirth, kept an eye to his own interest, and sweetened the severity with which he exacted his "dues" by a manner at once jocose and familiar. If a wealthy farmer had a child to christen, his reverence declined baptizing it in the chapel, but as a proof of his marked respect for its parents, he and his curate did them the honor of performing the ceremony at their own house. If a marriage was to be solemnized, provided the parties were wealthy, he adopted the same course, and manifested the same flattering marks of his particular esteem for the parties, by attending at their residence; or if they preferred the pleasure of a journey to his own house, he and his curate accompanied them home from the same motives. This condescension, whilst it raised the pride of the parties, secured a good dinner and a pleasant evening's entertainment for the priests, enhanced their humility exceedingly, for the more they enjoyed themselves, the more highly did their friends consider themselves honored. This mode of life might, one would suppose, lessen their importance and that personal respect which is entertained for the priests by the people; but it is not so—the priests can, the moment such scenes are ended, pass, with the greatest aptitude of habit, into the hard, gloomy character of men who are replete with profound knowledge, exalted piety, and extraordinary power. The sullen frown, the angry glance, or the mysterious allusion to the omnipotent authority of the church, as vested in their persons, joined to some unintelligible dogma, laid down as their authority, are always sufficient to check anything derogatory towards them, which is apt to originate in the unguarded moments of conviviality.

"Plase your Reverence, I'll put him up myself," said Denis to Father Finnerty, as he took his horse by the bridle, and led him towards the stable, "and how is my cowlt doin' wid you, sir?"

"Troublesome, Denis; he was in a bad state when I got him, and he'll cost me nearly his price before I have him thoroughly broke."

"He was pretty well broke wid me, I know," replied Denis, "and I'm afear'd you've given him into the hands of some one that knows little about horses. Mave," he shouted, passing the kitchen door, "here's Father Finnerty—go in, Docthor, and put big Brian Buie out o' the corner; for goodness sake Exltimnicate him from the hob—an' sure you have power to do that any way."

The priest laughed, but immediately assuming a grave face, as he entered, exclaimed—

"Brian Buie, in the name of the forty-seventh proposition of Euclid's Elements—in the name of the cube and square roots—of Algebra, Mathematics, Fluxions, and the doctrine of all essential spirits that admit of proof—in the name of Nebuchadanezar the divine, who invented the convenient scheme of taking a cold collation under a hedge—by the power of that profound branch of learning, the Greek Digemma—by the authority of true Latin, primo, of Beotian Greek, secundo, and of Arabian Hebrew, tertio; which is, when united by the skill of profound erudition, primo, secundo, tertio; or, being reversed by the logic of illustration, *tertio, secundo, primo. Commando te in nomine botteli potheeni boni drinkandi his oedibus, hac note, inter amicos excellentissimi amici mei, Dionissii O'Shaughnessy, quem beknavavi ex excellentissimo colto ejus, causa pedantissimi filii ejus, designali ecclesea, patri, sed nequaquam deo, nec naturae, nec ingenio;—commando te inquam, Bernarde Buie, surgere, stare, ambulare, et decedere e cornero isto vel hobbo, qua nunc sedes!* Yes, I command thee, Brian Buie, who sit upon the hob of my worthy and most excellent friend and parishioner, Denis O'Shaughnessy, to rise, to stand up before your spiritual superior, to walk down from it, and to tremble as if you were about to sink into the earth to the neck, but no further; before the fulminations of him who can wield the thunder of that mighty Salmoneus, his holiness the Pope, successor to St. Peter, who left the servant of the Centurion earless—I command and objurgate thee, sinner as thou art, to vacate your seat on the hob for the man of sancity, whose legitimate possession it is, otherwise I shall send you, like that worthy archbishop, the aforesaid Nebuchadanezar, to live upon leeks for seven years in the renowned kingdom of Wales, where the leeks may be seen to this day! Presto!"

These words, pronounced with a grave face, in a loud, rapid, and sonorous tone of voice, startled the good people of the house, who sat mute and astonished at such an exordium from the worthy pastor: but no sooner had he uttered Brian Buie's name, giving him, at the same time, a fierce and authoritative look, than the latter started to his feet, and stepped down in a kind of alarm towards the door. The priest immediately placed his hand upon his shoulder in a mysterious manner, exclaiming—

"Don't be alarmed, Brian, I have taken the force of the anathema off you; your power to sit or stand, or go where you please, is returned again. I wanted your seat, and Denis desired, me to excommunicate you out of it, which I did, and you accordingly left it without your own knowledge, consent, or power; I transferred you to where you stand, and you had no more strength to resist me than if you were an infant not three hours in the world!"

"I ax God's pardon, an' your Reverence's," said Brian, in a tremor, "if I have given offince. Now, bless my soul! what's this? As sure as I stand before you, neighbors, I know neither act nor part of how I was brought from the hob at all—neither act nor part! Did any of yez see me lavin' it; or how did I come here—can you tell me?"

"Paddy," said one of his friends, "did you see him?"

"The sorra one o' me seen him," replied Paddy: "I was lookin' at his Reverence, sthrivin' to know what he was sayin'."

"Pether, did you?" another inquired. "Me! I never seen a stim of him till he was standin' alone on the flure! Sure, when he didn't see or find himself goin', how could another see him?"

"Glory be to God!" exclaimed Mave; "one ought to think well what they say, when they spake of the clargy, for they don't know what it may bring down upon them, sooner or later!"

"Our Denis will be able to do that yet," said Susan to her elder sister.

"To be sure he will, girsha, as soon as he's ordained—every bit as well as Father Finnerty," replied Mary.

The young enthusiast's countenance brightened as her sister spoke: her dark eye became for a minute or two fixed upon vacancy, during which it flashed several times; until, as the images of her brother's future glory passed before her imagination; she became wrapt—her lip quivered—her cheek flushed into a deeper color, and the tears burst in gushes from her eyes.

The mother, who was now engaged in welcoming Father Finnerty—a duty which the priest's comic miracle prevented her from performing sooner—did not perceive her daughter's agitation, nor, in fact, did any one present understand its cause. Whilst the priest was taking Brian Buie's seat, she went once more to watch the return of Denis; and while she stood upon the stile, her father, after having put up the horse, entered the house, "to keep his Reverence company."

"An' pray, Docthor," he inquired, "where is Father Molony, that he's not wid you? I hope he won't disappoint us; he's a mighty pleasant gintleman of an evenin', an', barrin' your Reverence, I don't know a man tells a better story."

"He entreated permission from me this morning," replied Father Finnerty, "and that was leave to pay a visit to the Bishop, for what purpose I know not, unless to put in a word in season for the first parish that becomes vacant."

"Throth, an' he well desarves a parish," replied Denis; "an' although we'd be loath to part wid him, still we'd be proud to hear of his promotion."

"He'll meet Denis there," observed Susan, who had returned from the stile: "he'll be apt to be present at his trial wid the Bishop; an' maybe he'll be home along wid him. I'll go an' thry if I can see them agin;" and she flew out once more to watch their return.

"Now, Father Finnerty," said an uncle of Denis's, "you can give a good guess at what a dacent parish ought to be worth to a parish priest?"

"Mrs. O'Shaughnessy," said the priest, "is that fat brown goose suspended before the fire, of your own rearing?"

"Indeed it is, plase your Reverence; but as far as good male an phaties could go for the last month, it got the benefit of them."

"And pray, Mrs. O'Shaughnessy, have you many of the same kidney? I only ask for information, as I said to Peery Hacket's wife, the last day I held the Station in Peery's. There was just such another goose hanging before the fire; but, you must know, the cream of the joke was, that I had been after coming from the confessional, as hungry as a man could conveniently wish himself; and seeing the brown fat goose before the fire just as that is, why my teeth, Mave, began to get lachrymose. Upon my Priesthood it was such a goose as a priest's corpse might get up on its elbow to look at, and exclaim, 'avourneen machree, it's a thousand pities that I'm not living to have a cut at you!'—ha, ha, ha! God be good to old Friar Hennessy, I have that joke from him.

"'Well, Mrs. Hacket,' says I, as I was airing my fingers at the fire, 'I dare say you haven't another goose like this about the house? Now, tell me, like an honest woman, have you any of the same kidney?—I only ask for information.'

"Mrs. Hacket, however, told me she believed there might be a few of the same kind straggling about the place, but said nothing further upon it, until the Saturday following, when her son brings me down a pair of the fattest geese I ever cut up for my Sunday's dinner. Now, Mrs. O'Shaughnessy, wasn't that doing the thing dacent?"

"Well, well, Docthor," said Denis, "that was all right; let Mave alone, an' maybe she'll be apt to find out a pair that will match Mrs. Hacket's. Not that I say it, but she doesn't like to be outdone in anything."

"Docthor, I was wishin' to know, sir," continued the uncle of the absent candidate, "what the value of a good parish might be."

"I think, Mave, there's a discrepancy between the goose and the shoulder of mutton. The fact is, that if it be a disputation between them, as to which will be roasted first, I pronounce that the goose will have it. It's now, let me see, half past four o'clock, and, in my opinion, it will take a full half hour to bring up the mutton. So Mave, if you'll be guided by your priest, advance the mutton towards the fire about two inches, and keep the little girsha basting steadily, and then you'll be sure to have it rich and juicy."

"Docthor, wid submission, I was wantin' to know what a good parish might be—"

"Mike Lawdher, if I don't mistake, you ought to have good grazing down in your meadows at Ballinard. What will you be charging for a month or two's grass for this colt I've bought from my dacent friend, Denis O'Shaughnessy, here? And, Mike, be rasonable upon a poor man, for we're all poor, being only tolerated by the state we live under, and ought not, of course, to be hard upon one another."

"An' what did he cost you, Docthor?" replied Mike, answering one question by another; "what did you get for him, Denis?" he continued, referring for information to Denis, to whom, on reflection, he thought it more decorous to put the question.

Denis, however, felt the peculiar delicacy of his situation, and looked at the priest, whilst the latter, under a momentary embarrassment, looked significantly at Denis. His Reverence, however, was seldom at a loss.

"What would you take him to be worth, Mike?" he asked; "remember he's but badly trained, and I'm sure it will cost me both money and trouble to make anything dacent out of him."

"If you got him somewhere between five and twenty and thirty guineas, I would say you have good value for your money, plase your Reverence. What do you say, Denis—am I near it?"

"Why, Mike, you know as much about a horse as you do about the Pentateuch or Paralipomenon. Five and twenty guineas, indeed! I hope you won't set your grass as you would sell your horses."

"Why, thin, if your Reverence ped ready money for him, I maintain he was as well worth twenty guineas as a thief's worth the gallows; an' you know, sir, I'd be long sorry to differ wid you. Am I near it now, Docthor?"

"Denis got for the horse more than that," said his Reverence, "and he may speak for himself."

"Thrue for you, sir," replied Denis; "I surely got above twenty guineas for him, an' I'm well satisfied wid the bargain."

"You hear that now, Mike—you hear what he says."

"There's no goin' beyant it," returned Mike; "the proof o' the puddin' is in the atin,' as we'll soon know, Mave—eh, Docthor?"

"I never knew Mave to make a bad one," said the priest, "except upon the day Friar Hennessy dined with me here—my curate was sick, and I had to call in the Friar to assist me at confession; however, to do Mave justice, it was not her fault, for the Friar drowned the pudding, which was originally a good one, with a deluge of strong whiskey."

"'It's too gross,' said the facetious Friar, in his loud, strong voice—'it's too gross, Docthor Finnerty, so let us spiritualize it, that it may be Christian atin, fit for pious men to digest,' and then he came out with his thundering laugh—oigh, oigh, oigh, oigh! but he had consequently the most of the pudding to himself, an' indeed brought the better half of it home in his saddle-bags."

"Faix, an' he did," said Mave, "an' a fat goose that he coaxed Mary to kill for him unknownst to us all, in the coorse o' the day."

"How long is he dead, Docthor?" said Denis; "God rest him any way, he's happy!"

"He died in the hot summer, now nine years about June last; and talking about him, reminds me of a trick he put on me about two years before his death. He and I had not been on good terms for long enough before that time; but as the curate I had was then sickly, and as I wouldn't be allowed two, I found that it might be convenient to call in the Friar occasionally, a regulation he did not at all relish, for he said he could make far more by questing and poaching about among the old women of the parish, with whom he was a great favorite, in consequence of the Latin hymns he used to sing for them, and the great cures he used to perform—a species of devotion which neither I nor my curate had time to practise. So, in order to renew my intimacy, I sent him a bag of oatmeal and a couple of flitches of bacon, both of which he readily accepted, and came down to me on the following day to borrow three guineas. After attempting to evade him—for, in fact, I had not the money to spare—he at length succeeded in getting them from me, on the condition that he was to give my curate's horse and mine a month's grass, by way of compensation, for I knew that to expect payment from him was next to going for piety to a parson.

"'I will,' said he, 'give your horses the run of my best field'—for he held a comfortable bit of ground; 'but,' he added, 'as you have been always cutting at me about my principle, I must insist, if it was only to convince you of my ginerosity, that you'll lave the choosing of the month to myself.'

"As I really wanted an assistant at the time, in consequence of my curate's illness, he had me bound, in some degree, to his own will. I accordingly gave him the money; but from that till the day of his death, he never sent for our horses, except when there was a foot and a half of snow on the ground, at which time he was certain to despatch a messenger for him, 'with Father Hennessy's compliments, and he requested Doctor Finnerty to send the horses to Father Hennessy's field, to ate their month's grass.'"

"But is it true, Docthor, that his face was shinin' after his death?"

"True enough, and to my own knowledge, long before that event."

"Dear me," exclaimed Mave, "he was a holy man afther all!"

"Undoubtedly he was," said the priest; "there are spots in the sun, Mrs. O'Shaugh-nessy—we are not all immaculate. There never was one sent into this world without less or more sin upon them. Even the saints themselves had venial touches about them, but nothing to signify."

"Docthor," said the uncle, pertinaciously adhering to the original question, "you have an opportunity of knowin' what a good parish might be worth to a smart, active priest? For the sake of a son of mine that I've some notion of—"

"By the by, I wonder Denis is not here before now," exclaimed his Reverence, lending a deaf ear to Mike O'Shaughnessy's interrogatory.

Old Denis's favorite topic had been started, and he accordingly launched out upon it with all the delight and ardor of a fond father.

"Now, Docthor dear, before us all—an' sure you know as well as I do, that we're all friends together—what's your downright opinion of Denis? Is he as bright as you tould me the other mornin' he was?"

"Really, Denis O'Shaughnessy," replied his Reverence, "it's not pleasant to me to be pressed so often to eulogize a young gintleman of whose talents I have so frequently expressed my opinion. Is not once sufficient for me to say what

I've said concerning him? But, as we are all present, I now say and declare, that my opinion of Denis O'Shaughnessy, jun., is decidedly *peculiar*—decidedly.

"Come, girsha, keep basting the mutton, and never heed my boots—turn it about and baste the back of it better."

"God be thanked," exclaimed the delighted father, "sure it's comfort to hear that, any how—afther all the pains and throuble we've taken wid him, to know it's not lost. Why, that boy was so smart, Docthor, that, may I never sin, when he went first to the Latin, but—an' this no lie, for I have it from his own lips—when he'd look upon his task two or three times over night, he'd waken wid every word of it, pat off the book the next mornin'. And how do you think he got it? Why, the crathur, you see, used to dhrame that he was readin' it off, and so he used to get it that way in his sleep!"

At this moment Darby Moran, Denis's old foe entered, and his reception was cordial, and, if the truth were known, almost magnanimous on the part of Denis.

"Darby Moran," said he, "not a man, barrin' his Reverence here, in the parish we sit in, that I'm prouder to see on my flure—give me your hand, man alive, and Mave and all of ye welcome him. Everything of what you know is buried between us, and you're bound to welcome him, if it was only in regard of the handsome way he spoke of our son this day—here's my own chair, Darby, and sit down."

"Throth," said Darby, after shaking hands with the priest and greeting the rest of the company, "the same boy no one could spake ill of; and, although we and his people were not upon the best footin', still the sarra one o' me but always gave him his due."

"Indeed, I believe you, Darby," said his father; "but are you comfortable? Draw your chair nearer the fire—the evenin's gettin' cowld."

"I'm very well, Denis, I thank you;—nearer the fire! Faix, except you want to have me roasted along wid that shoulder of mutton and goose, I think I can't go much nearer it."

"I'm sorry, you wasn't in sooner, Darby, till you'd hear what Docthor Finnerty here—God spare him long among us—said of Denis a while ago. Docthor, if it wouldn't be makin' too free, maybe you'd oblage me wid repatin' it over again?"

"I can never have any hesitation," replied the priest, "in repeating anything to his advantage—I stated, Darby, that young Misther O'Shaughnessy was a youth of whom my opinion was decidedly *peculiar*—keep basting; child, you're forgetting the goose now; did you never see a priest's boots before?"

"An' nobody has a better right to know nor yourself, wherever larnin' and education's consarned," said the father.

"Why, it's not long since I examined him myself; I say it sitting here, and I believe every one that hears me is present; and during the course of the examination I was really astonished. The translations, and derivations, and conjugations, and ratiocinations, and variations, and investigations that he gave, were all the most remarkably original I ever heard. He would not be contented with the common sense of a passage; but he'd keep hunting, and hawking, and fishing about for something that was out of the ordinary course of reading, that I was truly struck with his eccentric turn of genius."

"You think he'll pass the Bishop with great credit, Docthor?"

"I'll tell you what I think, Denis—which is going further than I went yet—I think that if he were the Bishop, and the Bishop the candidate for Maynooth, that his lordship would have but a poor chance of passing. There's the pinnacle of my eulogium upon him; and now, to give my opinion on another important subject; I pronounce both the goose and mutton done to a turn. As it appears that Mrs. O'Shaughnessy has every other portion of the dinner ready, I move that we commence operations as soon as possible."

"But Denis, Docthor? it would be a pleasure to me to have him, poor fellow, wid all his throuble over, and his mind at ase; maybe if we wait a weeshy while longer, Docthor, that he'll come, and you know Father Molony too is to come yet, and some more of our friends."

"If the examination was a long one, I tell you that Mr. O'Shaughnessy may not be here this hour to come; and you may be sure, the Bishop, meeting such a bright boy, wouldn't make it a short one. As for Father Molony, he'll be here time enough, so I move again that we attack the citadel."

"Well, well, never say it again—the sarra one o' me will keep it back, myself bein' as ripe as any of you, barrin' his Reverence, that we're not to take the foreway of in anything. Ha! ha! ha!"

Whilst Mave and her daughters were engaged in laying dinner, and in making all the other arrangements necessary for their comfort, the priest took Denis aside, and thus addressed him:—

"Denis, I need scarcely remark that this meeting of our friends is upon no common occasion; that it's neither a wedding, nor a Station, nor a christening, but a gathering of relations for a more honorable purpose than any of them, excepting the Station, which you know is a religious rite. I just mention this privately, lest you might not be properly on your guard, and to prevent any appearance of maneness; or—in short, I hope you have abundance of everything; I hope you have, and that, not for your own sake so much as for that of your son. Remember your boy, and what he's designed for, and don't let the dinner or its concomitants be discreditable to him; for, in fact, it's his dinner, observe, and not yours."

"I'm thankful, I'm deeply thankful, an' for ever oblaged to your Reverence for your kindness; although, widout at all makin' little of it, it wasn't wanted here; never fear, Docthor, there'll be lashings and lavins."

"Well, but make that clear, Denis; here now are near two dozen of us, and you say there are more to come, and all the provision I see for them is a shoulder of mutton, a goose, and something in that large pot on the fire, which I suppose is hung beef."

"Thrue for you, sir, but you don't know that we've got a tarin' fire down in the barn, where there's two geese more and two shouldhers of mutton to help what you seen—not to mintion a great big puddin', an' lots of other things. Sure you might notice Mave and the girls runnin' in an' out to attind the cookin' of it."

"Enough, Denis, that's sufficient; and now, between you and me, I say your son will be the load-star of Maynooth, winch out-tops anything I said of him yet."

"There's a whole keg of whiskey, Docthor."

"I see nothing, to prevent him from being a bishop; indeed, it's almost certain, for he can't be kept back."

"I only hope your Reverence will be livin' when he praches his first sarmon. I have the dam of the coult still, an a wink's as good as a nod, please your Reverence."

"A strong letter in his favor to the President of Maynooth will do him no harm," said the priest.

They then joined their other friends, and in a few minutes an excellent dinner, plain and abundant, was spread out upon the table. It consisted of the usual materials which constitute an Irish feast in the house of a wealthy farmer, whose pride it is to compel every guest to eat so long as he can swallow a morsel. There were geese and fowl of all kinds—shoulders of mutton, laughing-potatoes, carrots, parsnips, and cabbage, together with an immense pudding, boiled in a clean sheet, and ingeniously kept together with long straws[4] drawn through it in all directions. A lord or duke might be senseless enough to look upon such a substantial, yeoman-like meal with a sneer; but with all their wealth and elegance, perhaps they might envy the health and appetite of those who partook of it. When Father Finnerty had given a short grace, and the operations of the table were commenced,—Denis looked around him with a disappointed air, and exclaimed:

"Father Finnerty, there's only one thing, indeed I may say two, a wantin' to complate our happiness—I mean Denis and Father Molony! What on earth does your Reverence think can keep them?"

To this he received not a syllable of reply, nor did he consider it necessary to urge the question any further at present. Father Finnerty's powers of conversation seemed to have abandoned him; for, although there were some few expressions loosely dropped, yet the worthy priest maintained an obstinate silence.

At length, in due time, he began to let fall an occasional remark, impeded considerably by hiccups, and an odd *Deo Gratias*, or *Laus Deo*, uttered in that indecisive manner which indicates the position of a man who debates within himself whether he ought to rest satisfied or not.

At this moment the tramping of a horse was heard approaching the door, and immediately every one of Denis's family ran out to ascertain whether it was the young candidate. Loud and clamorous was their joy on finding that they

---

[4] This, about thirty years ago, was usual at weddings and other feasts, where everything went upon a large scale.

were not mistaken; he was alone, and, on arriving at the door, dismounted slowly, and received their welcomes and congratulations with a philosophy which perplexed them not a little. The scene of confusion which followed his entrance into the house could scarcely be conceived: every hand was thrust out to welcome him, and every tongue loud in wishing him joy and happiness. The chairs and stools were overturned as they stood in the way of those who wished to approach him; plates fell in the bustle, and wooden trenchers trundled along the ground; the dogs, on mingling with the crowd that surrounded him, were kicked angrily from among them by those who had not yet got shaking hands with Denis. Father Finnerty, during this commotion, kept his seat in the most dignified manner; but the moment it had subsided he stretched out his hand to Denis, exclaiming:

"Mr. O'Shaughnessy, I congratulate you upon the event of this auspicious day! I wish you joy and happiness!"

"So do we all, over and over agin!" they exclaimed; "a proud gintleman he may be this night!"

"I thank you, Father Finnerty," said Denis, "and I thank you all!"

"Denis, avourneen," said his mother, "sit down an' ate a hearty dinner; you must be both tired and hungry, so sit down, avick, and when you're done you can tell us all."

"*Bonum concilium, mi chare Dionysi*—the advice is good, Mrs. O'Shaughnessy, and I myself will, in honor of this day, although I have already dined, just take another slice;" and as he spoke he helped himself. "Anything to honor a friend," he continued; "but, by the by, before I commence, I will try your own prescription, Denis—a whetter of this poteen at intervals. Hoch, that's glorious stuff—pure as any one of the cardinal virtues, and strong as fortitude, which is the champion of them all."

Denis, during these pleasant observations of the priest, sat silent, with a countenance pale and apparently dejected. When his mother had filled his plate, he gently put it away from him; but poured out a little spirits and water, which he drank.

"I cannot eat a morsel," said he; "mother, don't press me, it's impossible. We are all assembled here—friends, neighbors, and relations—I'll not disguise the fact—but the truth is, I have been badly treated this day; I have been, in the most barefaced manner, rejected by the Bishop, and a nephew of Father Molony's elected in my place."

The effect which this disclosure produced upon the company present, especially upon his own family, utterly defies description. His father hastily laid down his glass, and his eyes opened to the utmost stretch of their lids; his mother let a plate fall which she was in the act of handing to one of her daughters, who was about to help a poor beggar at the door; all convivial enjoyment was suspended; the priest laid down his knife and fork, and fixed his large eyes upon Denis, with his mouth full; his young sister, Susan, flew over to his side, and looked intensely into his countenance for an explanation of what he meant, for she had not properly understood him.

"Rejected!" exclaimed the priest—"rejected! Young man, I am your spiritual superior, and I command you, on this occasion, to practise no jocularity whatsoever—I lay it upon you as a religious duty to be serious and candid, to speak truth, and inform us at once whether what you have advanced be true or not?"

"I wish," said Denis, "that it was only jocularity on my part; but I solemnly assure you all that it is not. The Bishop told me that I suffered myself to be misled as to my qualifications for entrance; he says it will take a year and a half's hard study to enable me to matriculate with a good grace. I told him that your Reverence examined me, and said I was well prepared; and he said to me, in reply, that your Reverence was very little of a judge as to my fitness."

"Very well," said the priest, "I thank his lordship; 'tis true, I deserved that from him; but it can't be helped. I see, at all events, how the land lies. Denis O'Shaughnessy, I pronounce you to be, in the first place, an extremely stultified and indiscreet young man; and, in the next place, as badly treated and as oppressed a candidate for Maynooth as entered it. I pronounce you, in the face of the world, right well prepared for it; but I see now who is the spy of the diocese—oh, oh, thank you, Misther Molony—I now remimber, that he is related to his lordship through the beggarly clan of the M——'s. But wait a little; if I have failed here, thank Heaven I have interest in the next diocese, the Bishop of which is my cousin, and we will yet have a tug for it."

The mother and sisters of Denis were now drowned in tears; and the grief of his sister Susan was absolutely hysterical. Old Denis's brow became pale and sorrowful, his eye sunk, and his hand trembled. His friends all partook of this serious disappointment, and sat in silence and embarrassment around the table. Young Denis's distress was truly intense: he could not eat a morsel; his voice was tremulous with vexation; and, indeed, altogether the aspect of those present betokened the occurrence of some grievous affliction.

"Well," said Brian, Denis's elder brother, "I only say this, that it's a good story for him to tell that he is a Bishop, otherwise I'd think no more of puttin' a bullet through him from behind a hedge, than I would of shootin' a cur dog."

"Don't say that, Brian," said his mother; "bad as it is, he's one of our clargy, so don't spake disrespectful of him; sure a year is not much to wait, an' the next time you go before him it won't be in his power to keep you back. As for Father Molony, we wish, him well, but undher the roof of this house, except at a Station, or something else of the kind, he will never sit, barrin' I thought it was either dhry or hungry, that I wouldn't bring evil upon my substance by refusin' him."

"And that was his lordship's character of me?" inquired the priest once more with chagrin.

"If that was not, perhaps you will find it in this letter," replied Denis, handing him a written communication from the Bishop. Father Finnerty hastily broke open the seal, and read silently as follows:—

"*To the Rev. Father Finnerty, peace, and benediction.*

"Rev. Sir,

"I feel deep indignation at hearing the disclosure made to me this day by the bearer, touching your negotiation with him and his family, concerning a horse, as the value paid by them to you for procuring the use of my influence in his favor; and I cannot sufficiently reprobate such a transaction, nor find terms strong enough in which to condemn the parties concerned in it. Sir, I repeat it, that such juggling is more reprehensible on your part than on theirs, and that it is doubly disrespectful to me, to suppose that I could be influenced by anything but merit in the candidates. I desire you will wait upon me to-morrow, when I hope you may be able to place the transaction in such a light as will raise you once more to the estimation in which I have always held you. There are three other candidates, one of whom is a relation of your excellent curate's; but I have as yet made no decision, so that the appointment is still open. In the meantime, I command you to send back the horse to his proper owner, as soon after the receipt of this as possible, for O'Shaughnessy must not be shackled by any such stipulations. I have now to ask your Christian forgiveness, for having, under the influence of temporary anger, spoken of you before this lad with disrespect. I hereby make restitution, and beg that you will forgive me, and remember me by name in your prayers, as I shall also name you in mine.

"I am, etc.,

"+ James M."

When Father Finnerty read this letter, his countenance gradually assumed an expression of the most irresistible humor; nothing could be more truly comic than the significant look he directed toward each individual of the O'Shaughnessys, not omitting even the little boy who had basted the goose, whom he patted on the head with that mechanical abstraction resulting from the occurrence of something highly agreeable. The cast of his features was now the more ludicrous, when contrasted with the rueful visage he presented on hearing the manner in which his character had been delineated by the Bishop. At length he laid himself back in his chair, and putting his hands to his sides, fairly laughed out loudly for near five minutes.

"Oh!" he exclaimed, "Dionysius, Dionysius, but you are the simple and unsophisticated youth! Oh, you *bocaun* of the wide earth, to come home with a long face upon you, telling us that you were rejected, and you not rejected."

"Not rejected!—not rejecet!—not rejeckset!—not raxjaxet!" they all exclaimed, attempting to pronounce the word as well as they could.

"For the sake of heaven above us, Docthor, don't keep us in doubt one minute longer," said old Denis.

"Follow me," said the priest, becoming instantly grave, "follow me, Dionysius; follow me Denis More, and Brian, all follow—follow me. I have news for you! My friends, we'll be back instantly."

They accordingly passed into another room, where they remained in close conference for about a quarter of an hour, after which they re-entered in the highest spirits.

"Come," said Denis, "Pether, go over, *abouchal*, to Andy Bradagh's for Larry Cassidy the piper—fly like a swallow, Pether, an' don't come without him. Mave, achora, all's right. Susy, you darlin', dhry your eyes, avourneen, all's right. Nabors, friends—fill, fill—I say all's right still. My son's not disgraced, nor he won't be disgraced whilst I have a house over my head, or a beast in my stable. Docthor, reverend Docthor, drink; may I never sin, but you must get merry an' dance a 'cut-along' wid myself, when the music comes, and you must thrip the priest in his boots wid Susy here afther. Excuse me, nabors—Docthor, you won't blame me, there's both joy and sorrow in these tears. I have had a good family of childhre, an' a faithful wife; an' Mave, achora, although time has laid his mark upon you as well as upon myself, and the locks are gray that wor once as black as a raven: yet, Mave, I seen the day, an' there's many livin' to prove it—ay, Mave, I seen the day when you wor worth lookin' at—the wild rose of Lisbuie she was called, Docthor. Well, Mave, I hope that my eyes may be closed by the hands I loved an' love so well—an' that's your own, *agrab machree*, an' Denis's."

"Whisht, Denis asthore," said Mave, wiping her eyes, "I hope I'll never see that day. Afther seein' Denis here, what we all hope him to be, the next thing I wish is, that I may never live to see my husband taken away from me, acushla; no, I hope God will take me to himself before that comes."

There is something touching in the burst of pathetic affection which springs strongly from the heart of a worthy couple, when, seated among their own family, the feelings of the husband and father, the wife and mother, overpower them. In this case, the feeling is always deep in proportion to the strength and purity of domestic affection; still it is checked by the melancholy satisfaction that our place is to be filled by those who are dear to us.

"But now," said the priest, "that the scent lies still warm, let me ask you, Dionysius, how the Bishop came to understand the compactum?"

"I really cannot undertake to say," replied Denis; "but if any man has an eye like a *basileus* he has. On finding, sir, that there was some defect in my responsive powers, he looked keenly at me, closing his piercing-eyes a little, and inquired upon what ground I had presented myself as a candidate. I would have sunk the compactum altogether, but for the eye. I suspended and hesitated a little, and at length told him that there was an understanding—a—a—kind of—in short, he squeezed the whole secret out o' me gradationally. You know the result!"

"Ah, Dionysius, you are yet an unfledged bird; but it matters little. All will be rectified soon."

"Arrah, Dinis," inquired his mother, "was it only takin' a rise out of us you wor all the time? Throth, myself's not the better of the fright you put me into."

"No," replied Denis, "the Bishop treated me harshly, I thought: he said I was not properly fit. 'You might pass,' said he, 'upon a particular occasion, or under peculiar circumstances; but it will take at least a year and a half's study to enable you to enter Maynooth as I would wish you. You may go home again,' said he; 'at present I have dismissed the subject.'

"After this, on meeting Father Molony, he told me that his cousin had passed, and that he would be soon sent up to Maynooth: so I concluded all hope was over with me; but I didn't then know what the letter to Father Finnerty contained. I now see that I may succeed still."

"You may and shall, Denis; but no thanks to Father Molony for that: however, I shall keep my eye upon the same curate, never fear. Well, let that pass, and now for harmony, conviviality, and friendship. Gentlemen, fill your glasses—I mean your respective vessels. Come, Denis More, let that porringer of yours be a brimmer. Ned Hanratty, charge your noggin. Darby, although your mug wants an ear, it can hold the full of it. Mrs. O'Shaughnessy, that old family cruiskeen ought to be with your husband: but no matther—*non constat*—Eh? Dionysi? Intelligible?"

"*Intelligo, domine.*"

"Here then is health, success, and prosperity to Mr. Dionysius O'Shaughnessy, jun.! May he soon be on the Retreat in the vivacious walls of that learned and sprightly seminary, Maynooth! [5]On the Retreat, I say, getting fat upon half a meal a day for the first week, fasting tightly against the grain, praying sincerely for a settin' at the king's mutton, and repenting thoroughly of his penitence!"

"Well, Docthor, that is a toast. Denis, have you nothing to say to that? Won't you stand up an' thank his Reverence, anyhow?"

"I am really too much oppressed with relaxation," said Denis, "to return thanks in that florid style which would become my pretensions. I cannot, however, but thank Father Finnerty for his ingenious and learned toast, which does equal honor to his head and heart, and I might superadd, to his intellects also; for in drinking toasts, my friends, I always elaborate a distinction between strength of head and strength of intellect. I now thank you all for having in so liberal a manner drunk my health; and in grateful return, I request you will once more fill your utensils, and learnedly drink—long life and a mitre to the Reverend Father Finnerty, of the Society of St. Dominick, Doctor of Divinity and Parochial Priest of this excellent parish!—*Propino tibi salutem, Doctor doctissime, reverendissime, et sanctissime; nec non omnibus amicis hic congregatis!*"

---

[5] This is a passage which I fear few general readers will understand without explanation; the meaning is this:—When a young-man first enters Maynooth College he devotes himself for the space of eight days to fasting and prayer, separating himself as much as possible from all society. He must review his whole life, and ascertain, it he can, whether he has ever left any sin of importance unconfessed, either knowingly or by an emission that was culpably negligent. After this examination, which must be both severe and strict, he makes what is called a General Confession; that is, he confesses all the sins he ever committed as far back and as accurately as he can recollect them. This being over, he enters upon his allotted duties as a student and in good sooth feels himself in admirable trim for "a set-in at the King's Mutton."

The priest's eye, during this speech, twinkled with humor; he saw clearly that Denis thoroughly understood the raillery of his toast, and that the compliment was well repaid. On this subject he did not wish, however, to proceed further, and his object now was, that the evening should pass off as agreeably as possible.

Next morning Father Finnerty paid Denis a timely visit, having first, as he had been directed, sent home the colt a little after day-break. They then took an early breakfast, and after about half an hour's further deliberation, the priest, old Denis, and his son—the last mounted upon the redoubtable colt—proceeded to the Bishop's residence. His lordship had nearly finished breakfast, which he took in his study; but as he was engaged with his brother, the barrister, who slept at his house the night before, in order to attend a public meeting on that day, he could not be seen for some time after they arrived. At length they were admitted. The Right Reverend Doctor was still seated at the breakfast table, dressed in a morning-gown of fine black stuff, such as the brothers of the Franciscan order of monks usually wear, to which order he belonged. He wore black silk stockings, gold knee-buckles to his small-clothes, a rich ruby ring upon his finger, and a small gold cross, net with brilliants, about his neck. This last was not usually visible; but as he had not yet dressed for the day, it hung over his vest. He sat, or rather lolled back in a stuffed easy chair, one leg thrown indolently over the other. Though not an old man, he wore powder, which gave him an air of greater reverence; and as his features were sharp and intelligent, his eye small but keen, and his manner altogether impressive and gentlemanly, if not dignified, it was not surprising that Father Finnerty's two companions felt awed and embarrassed before him. Nor was the priest himself wholly free from that humbling sensation which one naturally feels when in the presence of a superior mind in a superior station of life.

"Good morning to your lordship!" said the priest, "I am exceedingly happy to see you look so well. Counsellor, your most obedient; I hope, sir, you are in good health!"

To this both gentlemen replied in the usual commonplace terms.

"Doctor," continued the priest, "this is a worthy dacent parishioner of mine, Denis O'Shaughnessy; and this is his son who has the honor to be already known to your lordship."

"Sit down, O'Shaughnessy," said the Bishop, "take a seat, young man."

"I humbly thank your lordship," replied Denis the elder, taking a chair as he spoke, and laying his hat beside him on the carpet. The son, who trembled at the moment from head to foot, did not sit as he was asked, but the father, after giving him a pluck, said in a whisper, "Can't you sit, when his lordship-bids you." He then took a seat, but appeared scarcely to know whether he sat or stood.

"By the by, Doctor, you have improved this place mightily," continued Father Finnerty, "since I had the pleasure of being here last. I thought I saw a green-house peeping over the garden-wall."

"Yes," replied the Bishop, "I am just beginning to make a collection of shrubs and flowers upon a small scale. I believe you are aware that tending and rearing flowers, Mr. Finnerty, is a favorite amusement with me."

"I believe I have a good right to know as much, Dr. M——," replied Mr. Finnerty.

"If I don't mistake, I sent you some specimens for your garden that were not contemptible. And if I don't mistake again, I shall be able to send your lordship a shrub that would take the pearl off a man's eye only to look at it. And what's more, it's quite a new-comer; not two years in the country."

"Pray how is it called, Mr. Finnerty."

"Upon my credit, Doctor, with great respect, I will tell you nothing more about it at present. If you wish to see it, or to know its name, or to get a slip of it, you must first come and eat a dinner with me. And, Counsellor, if you, too, could appear on your own behalf, so much the better."

"I fear I cannot, Mr. Finnerty, but I dare say my brother will do himself the pleasure of dining with you."

"It cannot be for at least six weeks, Mr. Finnerty," said the Bishop. "You forget that the confirmations begin in ten days; but I shall have the pleasure of dining with you when I come to confirm in your parish."

"Phoo! Why, Doctor, that's a matter of course. Couldn't your lordship make it convenient to come during the week, and bring the Counsellor here with you? Don't say no, Counsellor; I'll have no demurring."

"Mr. Finnerty," said the Bishop, "it is impossible at present. My brother goes to Dublin to-morrow, and I must go on the following day to attend the consecration of a chapel in the metropolis."

"Then upon my credit, your lordship will get neither the name nor description of my Facia, until you earn it by eating a dinner, and drinking a glass of claret with the Rev. Father Finnerty. Are those hard terms, Counsellor?—Ha! ha! ha! I'm not the man to put off a thing, I assure you."

"Mr. Finnerty," said the Bishop, smiling at, but not noticing the worthy priest's blunder about the Fucia, "if possible, I shall dine with you soon; but at present it is out of my power to appoint a day."

"Well, well, Doctor, make your own time of it; and now for the purport of our journey. Denis O'Shaughnessy here, my lord, is a warm, respectable parishioner of mine—a man indeed for whom I have a great regard. He is reported to have inherited from his worthy father, two horns filled with guineas. His grandmother, as he could well inform your lordship, was born with a lucky caul upon her, which caul is still in the family. Isn't it so, Denis?"

"My lord, in dignity, it's truth," replied Denis, "and from the time it came into the family they always thruv, thanks be to goodness!"

The lawyer sat eyeing the priest and Denis alternately, evidently puzzled to comprehend what such a remarkable introduction could lead to.

The Bishop seemed not to be surprised, for his features betrayed no change whatsoever.

"Having, therefore, had the necessary means of educating a son for the church, he has accordingly prepared this young man with much anxiety and expense for Maynooth."

"Plase your lordship," said Denis, "Docthor Finnerty is clothin' it betther than I could do. My heart is fixed upon seein' him what we all expect him to be, your lordship."

"Mr. Finnerty," observed the Bishop, "you seem to be intimately acquainted with O'Shaughnessy's circumstances; you appear to take a warm interest in the family, particularly in the success of his son."

"Undoubtedly my lord; I am particularly anxious for his success."

"You received my letter yesterday?"

"I am here to-day, my lord, in consequence of having received it. But, by the by, there was, under favor, a slight misconception on the part of your—"

"What misconception, sir!"

"Why, my lord—Counsellor, this is a—a—kind of charge his lordship is bringing against me, under a slight misconception. My lord, the fact is, that I didn't see what ecclesiastical right I had to prevent Denis here from disposing of his own property to—"

"I expect an apology from you, Mr. Finnerty, but neither a defence nor a justification. An attempt at either will not advance the interests of your young friend, believe me."

"Then I have only to say that the wish expressed in your lordship's letter has been complied with. But wait awhile, my lord," continued the priest, good-humoredly, "I shall soon turn the tables on yourself."

"How is that, pray?"

"Why, my lord, the horse is in your stable, and Denis declares he will not take him out of it."

"I have not the slightest objection to that," replied the Bishop, "upon the express condition that his son shall never enter Maynooth."

"For my part," observed Mr. Finnerty, "I leave the matter now between your lordship and O'Shaughnessy himself. You may act as you please, Doctor, and so may he."

"Mr. Finnerty, if I could suppose for a moment that the suggestion of thus influencing me originated with you, I would instantly deprive you of your parish, and make you assistant to your excellent curate, for whom I entertain a sincere regard. I have already expressed my opinion of the transaction alluded to in my letter. You have frequently offended me, Mr. Finnerty, by presuming too far upon my good temper, and by relying probably upon your own jocular disposition. Take care, sir, that you don't break down in some of your best jokes. I fear that under the guise of humor, you frequently avail yourself of the weakness, or ignorance, or simplicity of your parishioners. I hope, Mr. Finnerty, that while you laugh at the jest, they don't pay for it."

The priest here caught the Counsellor's eye, and gave him a dry wink, not unperceived, however, by the Bishop, who could scarcely repress a smile.

"You should have known me better, Mr. Finnerty, than to suppose that any motive could influence me in deciding upon the claims of candidates for Maynooth, besides their own moral character and literary acquirements. So long as I live, this, and this alone, shall be the rule of my conduct, touching persons in the circumstances of young O'Shaughnessy."

"My gracious lord," said Denis, "don't be angry wid Mr. Finnerty. I'll bear it all, for it was my fau't. The horse is mine, and say what you will, out of your stable I'll never bring him. I think, wid great sibmission a man may do what he pleases wid his own."

"Certainly," said the Bishop; "my consent to permit your son to goto Maynooth is my own. Now this consent I will not give if you press that mode of argument upon me."

"My Reverend Lord, as heaven's above me, I'd give all I'm worth to see the boy in Maynooth. If he doesn't go afther all our hopes, I'd break my heart." He was so deeply affected that the large tears rolled down his cheeks as he spoke.

"Will your Lordship buy the horse?" he added; "I don't want him, and you, maybe, do?"

"I do not want him," said the Bishop, "and if I did, I would not, under the present circumstances, purchase him from you."

"Then my boy won't get in, your lordship. And you'll neither buy the horse, nor take him as a present. My curse upon him for a horse! The first thing I'll do when I get home will be to put a bullet through him, for he has been an unlucky thief to us. Is my son aquil to the others, that came to pass your lordship?" asked Denis.

"There is none of them properly qualified," said the Bishop. "If there be any superiority among them your son has it. He is not without natural talent, Mr. Finnerty; his translations are strong and fluent, but ridiculously pedantic. That, however, is perhaps less his fault than the fault of those who instructed him."

"Are you anxious to dispose of the horse?" said the Counsellor.

"A single day, sir, he'll never pass in my stable," said Denis; "he has been an unlucky baste to me an' mine, an' to all that had anything to do wid him."

"Pray what age is he?"

"Risin' four, sir; 'deed I believe he's four all out, an' a purty devil's clip he is, as you'd wish to see."

"Come," said the Counsellor, rising, "let us have a look at him. Mr. Finnerty, you're an excellent judge; will you favor me with your opinion?"

The priest and he, accompanied by the two O'Shaughnessys, passed out to the stable yard, where their horses stood. As they went, Father Finnerty whispered to O'Shaughnessy:—

"Now, Denis, is your time. Strike while the iron is hot. Don't take a penny!—don't take a fraction! Get into a passion, and swear you'll shoot him unless he accepts him as a present. If he does, all's right; he can twine the Bishop round his finger."

"I see, sir," said Denis; "I see! Let me alone for managin' him."

The barrister was already engaged in examining the horse's mouth, as is usual, when the priest accosted him with—

"You are transgressing etiquette in this instance, Counsellor. You know the proverb—never look a gift horse in the mouth."

"How, Mr. Finnerty?—a gift horse!"

"His Reverence is right!" exclaimed Denis: "the sorra penny ever will cross my pocket for the same horse. You must take him as he stands, sir, barrin' the bridle an' saddle, that's not my own."

"He will take no money," said the priest.

"Nonsense, my dear sir! Why not take a fair price for him?"

"Divil the penny will cross my pocket for him, the unlucky thief!" replied the shrewd farmer.

"Then in that case the negotiation is ended," replied the barrister. "I certainly will not accept him as a present. Why should I? What claim have I on Mr. O'Shaughnessy?"

"I don't want you to take him," said Denis; "I want nobody to take him: but I know the dogs of the parish 'll be pickin' his bones afore night. You may as well have him, sir, as not."

"Is the man serious, Mr. Finnerty?"

"I never saw a man in my life having a more serious appearance, I assure you," said the priest.

"By Jove, it's a queer business," replied the other: "a most extraordinary affair as I ever witnessed! Why, it would be madness to destroy such a fine animal as that! The horse is an excellent one! However, I shall certainly not accept him, until I ascertain whether I can prevail upon the bishop to elect his son to this vacancy. If I can make the man no return for him, I shall let him go to the dogs."

"Go up and set to work," said the priest; "but remember that *tace* is Latin for a candle. Keep his lordship in the dark, otherwise this scion is ousted."

"True," said the other. "In the meantime bring them into the parlor until I try what can be done."

"Take the Bishop upon the father's affection for him," said the priest.

"You are right. I am glad you mentioned it."

"The poor man will break his heart," said the priest.

"He will," responded the Counsellor smiling.

"So will the mother, too," said the priest, with an arch look.

"And the whole family," replied the Counsellor.

"Go up instantly," said the priest; "you have often got a worse fee."

"And, perhaps, with less prospect of success," said the other. "Gentlemen, have the goodness to walk into the parlor for a few minutes, while I endeavor to soften my brother a little, if I can, upon this untoward business."

When the priest and his two friends entered the parlor, which was elegantly furnished, they stood for a moment to survey it.

Old Denis, however, was too much engaged in the subject which lay nearest his heart to take pleasure in anything else; at least until he should hear the priest's opinion upon the posture of affairs.

"What does your reverence think?" said Denis.

"Behave yourself," replied the pastor. "None of your nonsense! You know what I think as well as I do myself."

"But will Dionnisis pass?—Will he go to Maynooth?"

"Will you go to your dinner to-day, or to your bed to-night?"

"God be praised! Well, Docthor, wait till we see him off, then I'll be spakin' to you!"

"No," said the priest; "but wait till you tike a toss upon this sofa, and then you will get a taste of ecclesiastical luxury."

"Ay," said Denis, "but would it be right o' me to sit in it? Maybe it's consecrated."

"Faith, you may swear that; but it is to the ease and comfort of his lordship! Come, man, sit down, till you see how you'll sink in it."

"Oh, murdher!" exclaimed Denis, "where am I at all? Docthor dear, am I in sight? Do you see the crown o' my head, good or bad? Oh, may I never sin, but that's great state!—Well, to be sure!"

"Ay," said the priest, "see what it is to be a bishop in any church! The moment a man becomes a bishop, he fastens tooth and nail upon luxury, as if a mitre was a dispensation for enjoying the world that they have sworn to renounce. Dionysius, look about you! Isn't this worth studying for?"

"Yes," replied the hitherto silent candidate, "if it was perusal on the part of his lordship that got it."

"Upon my credit, a shrewd observation! Ah, Dionysius, merit is overlooked in every church, and in every profession; or perhaps—hem!—ehem!—perhaps some of your reverend friends might be higher up! I mean nobody; but if sound learning, and wit, and humor, together with several other virtues which I decline enumerating, could secure a mitre, why mitres might be on other brows."

"This is surely great state," observed the candidate; "and if it be a thing that I matriculate—"

"And yet," said the priest, interrupting him, "this same bishop—who is, no doubt, a worthy man, but who has no natural ear for a jest—was once upon a time the priest of an indifferent good parish, like myself; ay, and a poor, cowardly, culprit-looking candidate, ready to sink into the earth, before his bishop, like you."

"Me cowardly!" said the candidate: "I decline the insinuation altogether. It was nothing but veneration and respect, which you know we should entertain for all our spiritual superiors."

"That's truth decidedly; though, at the same time, your nerves were certainly rather entangled, like a ravelled hank. But no matter, man; we have all felt the same in our time. Did you observe how I managed the bishop?"

"I can't say I did," replied the candidate, who felt hurt at the imputation of cowardice before his father; "but I saw, sir, that the bishop managed you."

"Pray for a longer vision, Dionysius. I tell you that no other priest in the diocese could have got both you and me out of the dilemma in which we stood but myself. He has taken to the study of weeds and plants in his old days; and I, who have a natural taste for botany, know it is his weak side. I tell you, he would give the right of filling a vacancy in Maynooth, any day in the year, for a rare plant or flower. So much for your knowledge of human nature. You'll grant I managed the Counsellor?"

"Between my father and you, sir, things look well. We have not, however, got a certificate of success yet."

"*Patientia fit levior ferendo!*—Have patience, man. Wait till we see the Counsellor!"

He had scarcely uttered the last words when that gentleman entered.

"Well, Counsellor," said the priest, "is it a hit?"

"Pray what is your Christian name, Mr. O'Shaughnessy?" inquired the lawyer o! young Denis.

"My Christian name, sir," replied Denis, "is Di-o-ny-si-us O'Shaughnessy. That, sir, is the name by which I am always appellated."

"That's quite sufficient," said the other, "I shall be with you again in a few minutes."

"But won't you give us a hint, my good sir, as to how the land lies?" said the priest, as the lawyer left the room.

"Presently, Mr. Finnerty, presently."

"Intelligisme, Dionisi?"

"Vix, Domine. Quid sentis?"

"Quid sentis! No, but it was good fortune sent us. Don't you persave, Dionysius, and you, Denis—don't you know, I say, that this letter of admission couldn't be written except the bishop knew his name in full? Unlucky! Faith if ever a horse was lucky this is he."

"I declare, Docthor," said the father, "I can neither sit nor stand, nor think of any one thing for a minute, I'm so much on the fidgets to know what the Bishop 'ill say."

"I also," said Dionysius, "am in state of evaporation and uncertainty touching the same point. However, this I can affirm with veracity, that if I am rejected, my mind is made up to pursue an antithetical course of life altogether. If he rejects me now, he will never reject me again."

"Musha, how—Denny—Dionysis, avick? What do you mane?" said the father.

"I will give," said the son, "what is designated a loose translation of my meaning to Mr. Finnerty here, if I find that I am excluded on this occasion."

"And if you do succeed," said the priest, "I would advise you to hire a loose translator during the remainder of your residence among us; for upon my veracity, Dionysius, the King's English will perform hard duty until you enter Maynooth. Not a word under six feet will be brought into the ranks—grenadiers every one of them, not to mention the thumpers you will coin."

"Come, Docthor Finnerty," said our candidate, pulling up a little, "if the base Latin which you put into circulation were compared with my English thumpers, it would be found that of the two, I am more legitimate and etymological."

"I shall be happy to dispute that point with you another time," said the priest, "when we can—Silence, here comes the Counsellor."

"Mr. O'Shaughnessy," said the lawyer, addressing the candidate, "allow me to congratulate you on your success! Your business is accomplished. The Bishop is just finishing a letter for you to the President of Maynooth. I assure you, I feel great pleasure at your success."

"Accept my thanks, sir," said Denis, whose eye was instantly lit up with delight—"accept my most obsequious thanks to the very furthest extent of my gratitude."

The Barrister then shook hands with old Denis. "O'Shaughnessy," said he, "I am very happy that I have had it in my power to serve you and your son."

"Counsellor," said Denis, seizing his hand in both of his—"Counsellor, *ahagur machree* Counsellor, oh, what—what—can I say!—Is he—is it possible—is it thruth that my boy is to go to Maynewth this time? Oh, if you knew, but knew, the heavy, dead weight you tuck off o' my heart! Our son not cast aside—not disgraced!—for what else would the people think it? The horse!—a poor bit of a coult—a poor unsignified animal! To the devil wid him. What is he compared to the joy an' delight of this minute? Take him, sir; take him—an' if he was worth his weight in goold, I vow to Heaven above me, I'd not think him too good. Too good!—no, nor half good enough for you. God remember this to you! an' he will, too. Little you know the happiness you have given us, Counsellor! Little you know it. But no matther! An' you, too, Father Finnerty, helped to bring this about. But sure you were ever an' always our friend! Well, no matther—no matther! God will reward you both."

"My brother wishes me to see Mr. Finnerty and your son," said the barrister; "I think they had better go up to him. He is anxious to get a slip of your shrub, Mr. Finnerty."

"Ah, I thought so," said the priest—"I thought as much."

The Bishop, on their reappearance, presented Denis with the long wished-for letter. He then gave him a suitable exhortation with reference to the serious and responsible duties for which he was about to prejjare himself. After concluding his admonition, he addressed Father Finnerty as follows:

"Now Mr. Finnerty, this matter has ended in a manner satisfactory, not only to your young friend, but to yourself. You must promise me that there shall be no more horse-dealing. I do not think jockeying of that description either creditable or just. I am unwilling to use harsher language, but I could not conscientiously let it pass without reproof. In the next place, will you let me have a slip of that flowering shrub you boast of?"

"Doctor," said the priest, "is it possible you ask it of me? Why, I think your lordship ought to know that it's your own, as is every plant and flower in my garden that you fancy. Do you dine at home to-morrow, my lord?"

"I do," said the Bishop. "Well, then, I shall come up with a slip or two of it, and dine with you. I know the situation in which it grows best; and knowing this, I will put it down with my own hands. But I protest, my lord, against you allowing me to be traced in the business of the shrub at all, otherwise I shall have the whole county on my back."

"Be under no apprehension of that, Mr. Finnerty. I shall be happy if you dine with me; but bring it with you. How did you come to get it so early after its appearance in this country?"

"I got it from headquarters, Doctor—from one of the best botanists in the three kingdoms; certainly from the best Irish botanist living—my friend, Mr Mackay, of the College Botanic Gardens. My lord, I wish you good morning; but before I go, accept my thanks for your kindness to my young friend. I assure you he will be a useful man; for he is even now no indifferent casuist."

"And I, my lord," said Denis, "return you my most grateful—hem—my most grateful—and—most supercilious thanks for the favor—the stupendous favor you have conferred upon me."

"God bless you, my dear child," returned the bishop; "but if you be advised by me, speak more intelligibly. Use plain words, and discard all difficult and pedantic expressions. God bless you! Farewell!"

On coming down, they found old Denis in the stable-yard in rather a ridiculous kind of harness. The saddle that had been on the colt was strapped about him with the bridle, for both had been borrowed from a neighbor.

"Dionnisis an' I must both ride the same horse," said he, "an' as we have two saddles, I must carry one of them."

An altercation then ensued as to which should ride foremost. The son, now in high glee, insisted on the father's taking the seat of honor; but the father would not hear of this. The lad was, in his opinion, at least semi-clerical, and to ride behind would be a degradation to so learned a youth. They mounted at length, the son foremost, and the father on the crupper, the saddle strapped about him, with the stirrups dangling by the horse's flanks. Father Finnerty, who accompanied them, could not, however, on turning from the bishop's grounds into the highway, get a word out of them. The truth is, both their hearts were full; both were, therefore, silent, and thought every minute an hour until they reached home.

This was but natural. A man may conceal calamity or distress even from his dearest friends; for who is there who wishes to be thrust back from his acknowledged position in life? Or who, when he is thrust back, will not veil his misfortunes or his errors with the guise of indifference or simulation? In good fortune we act differently. It is a step advanced; an elevation gained; there is nothing to fear, or to be ashamed of, and we are strongly prompted by vanity to proclaim it to the world, as we are by pride to ascribe its occurrence to our own talents or virtues. There are other and purer motives for this. The affections will not be still; they seek the hearts to which they tend; and having found them, the mutual interchange of good takes place. Father Finnerty—whose heart, though a kind one, had, probably, been too long out of practice to remember the influence and working of the domestic affections—could not comprehend the singular conduct of the two O'Shaughnessys.

"What the devil is the matter with you?" he inquired. "Have you lost the use of your speech?"

"Push an' avourneen," said the father to Denis—"push an; lay the spur to him. Isn't your spur on the right foot?"

"Most certainly," said Denis, now as pedantic as ever—"most certainly it is. You are not to be informed that our family spur is a right-foot spur."

"Well, then, Peter Gallagher's spur that I have an is a left-foot spur, for it's an my left foot."

"You are a bright pair," said the priest, somewhat nettled at their neglect of him—"you are a bright pair, and deeply learned in spurs. Can't you ride asier?"

"Never heed him," said the father, in a whisper; "do you, give the mare the right spur, an' I'll give her the left. Push an! that's it."

They accordingly dashed forwrard, Denis plying, one heel, and the father another, until the priest found himself gradually falling behind. In vain he plied both spurs; in vain he whipped, and wriggled on the saddle, and pressed forwrard his hack. Being a priest's horse, the animal had been accustomed for the last twelve years to a certain jog-trot-pace, beyond which it neither would nor could go. On finding all his efforts to overtake them unsuccessful, he at last shouted after them.

"Do you call that gratitude, my worthy friends? To lave me creeping over the ups and downs of this villanous road without company?"

"Lay an, aroon," said the father. "Let us get home. Oh, how your poor mother will die with joy, an' Susy, an' Nanny, an' Brian, an' Michael, an' Dick, an' Lanty, an' all o' them. Glory be to Heaven! what a meetin' we'll have! An' the nabors, too! Push an' avick machree."

"My curse upon you, Friar Hennessy!" exclaimed the priest, in a soliloquy, "it was you who first taught this four-footed snail to go like a thief to the gallows. I wish to Heaven you had palmed him on some one else, for many a dinner I have lost by him in my time. Is that your gratitude, gentlemen? Do I deserve this?"

"What is he sayin'?" said the father.

"He is declaiming about gratitude," replied Denis.

"Lay-an' her," said the father. "Poor Mave!"

"Such conduct does you credit," shouted the priest. "It's just the way of the world. You have got what you wanted out of me, an' now you throw me off. However, go on."

"What's that?" said the father again.

"He is desiring us to go on,' replied the son.

"Then, in the name o' Goodness, do so, avourneen. Susy will die downright."

"Where am I to dine to-day?" shouted the priest, in a louder voice. "I say, where am I to come in for my dinner, for I'm not expected at home, and my curate dines out?"

"I can't hear him," said the father.

"He says the curate dines out; an' he wants to know if he's to dine with us."

"Throth, an' he won't; not that we begrudge it to him; but for this day the sarra one we'll have but our own relations. Push an. An' Brian, too, poor fellow, that was always so proud of you!"

They had now reached the top of an ascent on the road, whilst the priest toiled up after them. In a few minutes they began to descend, and consequently were out of his sight.

No description of mine could give an adequate perception to the reader of what was felt by the family on hearing that the object of Denis's hopes, and their own proud ambition, was at length accomplished. The Bishop's letter was looked at, turned in every direction, and the seal inspected with a kind of wonderful curiosity, such as a superstitious person would manifest on seeing and touching some sacred relic. The period appointed for his departure now depended upon the despatch with which they could equip him for college. But until this event should arrive, his friends lost no opportunity of having him among them. Various were the treats he got in fair and markets. Proud were his relations when paying' him the respect which he felt right sincere pleasure in receiving. The medium between dignity and humility which he hit off in these scenes, was worthy o'f being recorded; but, to do him justice, his forte lay in humility. He certainly condescended with a grace, and made them feel the honor done them by his vouchsafing to associate with such poor creatures as if he was one of themselves. To do them also justice, they appeared to feel his condescension; and, as a natural consequence, were ready to lick the very dust under his feet, considering him, as they did, a priest in everything but ordination.

Denis, besides his intercourse with humble relatives, was now asked to dine with the neighboring clergymen, and frequently made one at their parties. In the beginning, his high opinion and awe of the clerical character kept him remarkably dull and sheepish. Many an excellent joke was cracked at his expense; and often did he ask himself what Phadrick Murray, his father's family, or his acquaintances in general, would say, if they saw his learning and his logic so villanously degraded. In proportion, however, as conviviality developed among his reverend friends many defects, opinions, and failings, which he never suspected them to possess, so did he begin to gather courage and facility of expression. By degrees he proceeded modestly from the mild and timid effort at wit to the steadier nerve of moderate confidence—another step brought him to the indifference of a man who can bear an unsuccessful attempt at pleasantry, without being discomposed; the third and last stage advanced him to downright assurance, which having reached, he stopped at nothing. From this forward he began to retort upon his clerical companions, who found that the sheepish youth whom they had often made ridiculous, possessed skill, when properly excited, to foil them at their own weapons. He observed many things in their convivial meetings. The holy man, whom his flock looked upon as a being of the highest sanctity, when lit up into fun and frolic, Denis learned to estimate at his just value. He thought, besides, that a person resolved to go to heaven, had as good a chance of being saved by the direct mercy of God, as through the ministration of men, whose only spiritual advantage over himself consisted in the mere fact of being in orders. To be sure, he saw the usual exceptions among them that are to be found among every other class; but he drew his conclusions from the general rule. All this, however, failed in removing that fundamental principle of honest superstition in which he had been trained. The clergymen whom he saw were only a few who constituted the great body of the church; but when the long and sanctified calendar of saints and miracles opened upon him, there still remained enough to throw a dim and solemn charm of shadowy pomp around the visions of a mind naturally imaginative.

Messengers were once more sent abroad, to inform their friends of his triumph, who, on ascertaining that his journey was fixed for an early day, lost no time in pouring in, each with some gift suited to their circumstances. Some of these were certainly original, the appropriateness having been in every case determined by the wealth or poverty, ignorance, or knowledge, of those who offered them. Some poor relation, for instance, brought him a shirt or two of materials so coarse, that to wear it in a college would be out of the question; others offered him a pair of brogues, much too vulgar for the society he was about to enter; others, again, would present him with books—for it is not at all uncommon to find in many illiterate Irish families half-a-dozen old volumes of whose contents they are ignorant, lying in a dusty corner, where they are kept till some young scion shall be sufficiently instructed to peruse them. The names of these were singular enough. One presented him with "The Necessity of Penance;" another with "Laugh and be Fat;" a third with the "Key of Paradise;" a fourth with "Hell Open;" a fifth handed him a copy of the "Irish Rogues and Rapparees; a sixth gave him "Butler's Lives of Saints;" a seventh "The Necessity of Fasting;" an eighth "The Epicure's *Vade Mecum*." The list ran on very ludicrously. Among them were the "Garden of Love and Royal Flower of Fidelity;" "An Essay on the Virtue of Celibacy;" and another "On the Increase of Population in Ireland." To these we may add "The Devil upon Two Sticks," and "The Life of St. Anthony."

"Take these, Misther Denis," said the worthy souls; "they're of no use to us at all at all; but they'll sarve you, of coorse, where you're goin', bekase when you want books in the college you can use them."

Honest Phadrick Murray, in lieu of a more valuable present, brought him his wife's largest and best shawl as a pocket handkerchief.

"Katty, sir, sent you this," said Phadrick, "as a pocket handkerchy; an' be gorra, Mither Denis, if you begin at this corner, an' take it out o' the face, it'll last you six months at a time, any how."

Another neighbor came with a *cool* of rendered lard, hoping it might be serviceable.

"Norah, sir," said the honest friend who brought it, "sent you a' crock of her own lard. When, you're makin' colcanon, sir, or *sthilk*,⁶ in the college, if you slip in a lamp of this, it'll save you the price of bufther. The grace 'ill be useful to you, whether or not; an' they say there's a scarcity of it in the college.".

A third brought him an oak sapling to keep in his hand about the purlieus of the establishment.

"We know," said he, "that you're given to arguin' an' to that thing you call logic, Misther Denis. Now, sir, if you're ever hard set in an argument or the like o' that, or if any o' the shthudjeents 'ud be throuble-some or imperant, why give them a touch o' this—a lick of it, do you see; jist this a way. First come wid a back sthroke upon the left ear, if they want to be properly convinced; an' thin agin' afore they have time to recover, come down wid a visitation upon the kidney, My life for yours, they'll soon let you alone. Nothin' puzzles one in an argument more than it does."

"Ay," said Denis, "that is what they call—in the books the *argumentum baculinum*. I accept your present, Roger; but I flatter myself I shall be a match for any of the collegians without having recourse to the argumentum baculinum."

A poor old widow, who was distantly related to them, came upwards of four miles with two or three score of eggs, together with a cock and hen; the eggs for his own use, and the latter for breeding in Maynooth. "Avourneen, Misther O'Shaughnessy," said she, in broken English, "when you ate out all the eggs, maybe you could get a sonsy little corner about the collegian that you're goin' to larn to be a priest in, an' put them both into it; "—pointing at the same time to the cock and hen—"an' whishper," she continued, in a low friendly voice, "if you could get a weeshy wisp o' sthraw, an slip it undher your own bed, it would make a nest for them, an' they'd lay an egg for your breakfast all days in the year. But, achora, don't let them be widout a nest egg; an' whishper—maybe you'd breed a clackin' out o' them, that you might sell. Sure they'd help to buy duds of cloes for you; or you might make presents of the crathurs to the blessed an' holy collegian himself. Wouldn't it be good to have him an your side?—He'd help to make a gintleman of you, any way. Faix, sure he does it for many, they say. An' whishper—the breed, avourneen, is good; an' I'm not afeard to say that there never was sich a chicken in the whole collegian, as the ould cock himself. He's the darlin' all out, an' can crow so stoutly, that it bates the world. Sure his comb's a beauty to look at, the darlin'; an' only it's to yourself, an' in regard of the blessed place he's goin' to, I wouldn't part wid him to nobody whatsomever, at all, good or bad."

The most original gift of all was a purse, formed of a small bladder, ingeniously covered with silk. It was given to him by his uncle, as a

---

⁶ Sthilk is made by bruising a quantity of boiled Potatoes and beans together. The potatoes, however, having first been reduced to a pulpy state, the beans are but partially broken. It is then put into dish, and a pound of butter or rendered lard thrust into the middle of it.

remembrance of him, in the first place; and secondly, for a more special purpose.

"This will sarve you, sir," said his uncle, "an' I'll tell you how: if you want to smuggle in a sup of good whiskey—as of coorse you will, plase goodness—why this houlds exactly a pint, an' is the very thing for it. The sorra one among them will ever think of searchin' your purse, at least for whiskey. Put it in your pocket, Misther Dionmsis; an' I'd take it as a great kindness if you'd write me a scrape or two of the pen, mentionin' what a good parish 'ud be worth: you'll soon be able to tell me, for I've some notion myself of puttin' Barny to Latin."

Denis was perfectly aware of the honest warmth of heart with which these simple tokens of esteem were presented to him; and young as he was, his knowledge of their habits and prejudices prevented him from disappointing them by a refusal. He consequently accepted everything offered him, appropriated to himself whatever was suitable to his wants, converted the remainder into pocket-money, and, of course, kept his conscience void of offence toward them all: a state of Christian virtue which his refusal of any one gift would have rendered difficult.

On the day before his departure the friends and relations of the family assembled to hold their farewell meeting. The same spirit which marked all their rustic symposia presided in this; if we except a feeling of sorrow natural to his family on being separated from one they loved so affectionately. Denis, who was never deficient in warmth of feeling, could not be insensible to the love and pride with which his family had always looked upon him. Ambition, as he approached it, lost much of its fictitious glitter. A sense of sorrow, if not of remorse, for the fastidious and overbearing spirit he had manifested to them, pressed upon his heart. Pride, in fact, was expelled; nature resumed her empire over him; he looked upon the last two months of his life as a man would be apt to do who had been all that time under the dominion of a feverish dream. We do not say, however, that either ambition or superstition was thoroughly expelled from his mind; for it is hard at all times to root them out of the system of man: but they ceased to govern him altogether. A passion, too, as obstinate as either of them, was determined to dispute their power. The domestic affections softened his heart; but love, which ambition left for dead, was only stunned; it rose again, and finding a favorable position, set its seal to his feelings.

Denis himself, some days before that appointed for his departure, became perfectly conscious that his affections were strongly fixed upon Susan Connor. The nature of their last interview filled him with shame; nay, more, it inspired him with pity for the fair, artless girl whom he had so unfeelingly insulted. The manner in which he had won her young affections; the many tender interviews that had passed between them; the sacred promises of unchangeable love they had made to each other: all crowded to his imagination with a power which reduced his spiritual ambition and ecclesiastical pride, at least to the possession only of a divided empire. He had, therefore, with his book in his hand as usual, taken many solitary walks for the preceding few days, with the expectation of meeting Susan. He heard that for the last month or six weeks she had looked ill, been in low spirits, and lost her health. The cause of this change, though a secret to the world, was known to him. He knew, indeed, that an interview between them was indispensable; but had it not been so, we question whether he would have been able to leave home without seeing her.

His evening strolls, however, up until the day before his setting out for college, were fruitless. Susan, who heretofore had been in the habit of walking in the evenings among the green dells around her father's house, was ever since their last meeting almost invisible. In the meantime, as the day before that of his leaving the neighborhood had arrived, and as an interview with her was, in a religious point of view, essentially necessary, he took his book in the course of the evening, and by a path slightly circuitous, descended the valley that ran between his father's house and hers. With solemn strides he perambulated it in every direction—north, south, east, and west; not a natural bower in the glen was unexplored; not a green, quiet nook unsearched; not a shady tree unexamined; but all to no purpose. Yet, although he failed in meeting herself, a thousand objects brought her to his heart. Every dell, natural bower, and shady tree, presented him with a history of their past affections. Here was the spot where, with beating heart and crimson cheek, she had first breathed out in broken music the acknowledgment of her love; there had another stolen meeting, a thousand times the sweeter for being stolen, taken place. Every spot, in fact, was dear to him, and every object associated itself with delightful emotions that kindled new life in a spirit from which their parent affections had not yet passed away.

Denis now sought the only other place where he had any likelihood of meeting her: this was at the well below her father's house. He walked down along the banks of the little stream that ran past it, until he reached a thorn bush that grew within a few yards of the spring. Under this he sat, anxiously hoping that Susan might come to fill her evening pail, as he knew she was wont to do. A thick flowery branch of the hawthorn, for it was the latter end of May, hung down from the trunk, and served as a screen through which he could observe her should she appear, without being visible himself.

It was now the hour of twilight; the evening was warm and balmy; the whitethorn tinder which he sat, and the profusion of wild flowers that spangled the bosom of the green glen, breathed their fragrance around him, and steeped, the emotions and remembrances which crowded thickly on him in deep and exquisite tenderness. Up in the air he heard the quavering hum of the snipe, as it rose and fell in undulating motion, and the creak of the rail in many directions around him. From an adjoining meadow in the distance, the merry voices of the village children came upon his ear, as they gathered the wild honey which dropped like dew from the soft clouds upon the long grassy stalks, and meadow-sweet, on whose leaves it lay like amber. He remembered when he and Susan, on meeting there for a similar purpose, felt the first mysterious pleasure in being together, and the unaccountable melancholy produced by separation and absence.

At length he heard a footstep; but he could not persuade himself that the slow and lingering tread of the person approaching him was that of Susan, so much did it differ from the buoyant and elastic step with which she used to trip along. On looking through the branches, however, he perceived her coming towards him, carrying the pitcher as usual in her hand. The blood was already careering at full speed through his veins, and the palpitations of his heart were loud enough to be heard by the ear.

Oh, beauty, beauty! *terrima causa belli*, thou dost play the devil with the hearts of men! Who is there who doth not wish to look upon thee, from the saint to the sinner?—None. For thee worlds have been lost; nations swept off the earth; thrones overturned; and cities laid in ashes! Adam, David, Marc Antony, Abelard, and Denis O'Shaughnessy, exhibit histories of thy power never to be forgotten, but the greatest of these is Denis O'Shaughnessy.

Susan was about the middle size; her tresses, like those of the daughters of her country, were a fair brown, and abundant. Her features were not such, we admit, as mark regular and scientific perfection, and perhaps much of their power was owing to their not being altogether symmetrical. Her great charm consisted in a spirit of youthful innocence, so guileless that the very light of purity and truth seemed to break in radiance from her countenance. Her form was round, light, and flexible. When she smiled her face seemed to lose the character of its mortality—so seraphic and full of an indescribable spell were its lineaments; that is, the spell was felt by its thrilling influence upon the beholder, rather than by any extraordinary perception of her external beauty. The general expression of her countenance, however, was that of melancholy. No person could look upon her! white forehead and dark flashing eyes, without perceiving that she was full of tenderness and enthusiasm; but let the light of cheerfulness fall upon her face, and you wished never to see it beam with any other spirit. In her met those extremes of character peculiar to her country. Her laughing lips expanded with the playful delicacy of mirth, or breathed forth, with untaught melody and deep pathos, her national songs of sorrow.

A little before she made her appearance, the moon had risen and softened with her dewy light the calm secluded scene around them. Denis, too, had an opportunity of seeing the lovely girl more distinctly. Her dress was simple but becoming. Her hair, except the side ringlets that fell to heighten the beauty of her neck, was bound up with a comb which Denis himself had presented to her. She wore a white dimity bedgown, that sat close to her well-formed person, descended below her knee, and opened before; the sleeves of it did not reach the elbow, but displayed an arm that could not be surpassed for whiteness and beauty. The bedgown was frilled about the shoulder, which it covered, leaving the neck only, and the upper part of her snowy bosom, visible. A dark ribbon, tied about her waist, threw her figure into exquisite outline, and gave her that simple elegance which at once bespeaks the harmony of due proportion.

On reaching the well she filled her vessel, and placed it on a small mound beside her; then sitting down, she mused for some time, and turning her eyes towards Denis's father's sighed deeply.

"It's the least," said the humble girl, "that I may look towards the house that the only one I ever loved, or ever will love, lives in. Little I thought when I loved him that I was standin' between him an' God. Loved him! I wish I could say it was past. I wish I could: for I am afeared that till my weak heart breaks it will love him still. God pity me! It would be well for me I had never seen him! But why he should go to Maynooth without givin' me back my promise I cannot tell."

Denis rose and approached her. Susan, on seeing him, started, and her lover could perceive that she hastily wiped the tears from her eyes. A single glance, however, convinced her that it was he; and such was the guileless simplicity of her heart, joined to the force of habit, that her face beamed with one of her wonted smiles at his appearance. This soon passed away, and her features again resumed an expression of deep melancholy. Our hero now forgot his learning; his polysyllables were laid aside, and his pedantry utterly abandoned. His pride, too, was gone, and the petty pomp of artificial character thing aside like an unnecessary garment which only oppresses the wearer.

"Susan," said he, "I am sorry to see you look so pale and unhappy. I deeply regret it; and I could not permit this day to pass, without seeing and speaking to you. If I go to-morrow, Susan, may I now ask in what light will you remember me?"

"I'll remember you without anger, Denis; with sorrow will I remember you, but not, as I said, in anger; though God knows, and you know, the only token you lave me to remember you by is a broken heart."

"Susan," said Denis, "it was an unhappy attachment, as circumstances have turned out; and I wish for both our sakes we had never loved one another. For some time past my heart has been torn different ways, and, to tell you the truth, I acknowledge that within the last three or four months I have been little less than a villain to you."

"You speak harshly of yourself, Denis; I hope, more so than you deserve."

"No, Susy. With my heart fixed upon other hopes, I continued to draw your affections closer and closer to me."

"Well, that was wrong, Denis; but you loved me long before that time, an' it's not so asy a thing to draw away the heart from what we love; that is, to draw it away for ever, Denis, even although greater things may rise up before us."

As she pronounced the last words, her voice, which she evidently strove to keep firm, became unsteady.

"That's true, Susan, I know it; but I will never forgive myself for acting a double part to you and to the world. There is not a pang you suffer but ought to fall as a curse upon my head, for leading you into greater confidence, at a time when I was not seriously resolved to fulfil my vows to you."

"Denis," said the unsuspecting girl, "you're imposin' on yourself—you never could do so bad, so treacherous an act as that. No, you never could, Denis; an', above all the world, to a heart that loved and trusted you as mine did. I won't believe it, even from your own lips. You surely loved me, Denis, and in that case you couldn't be desateful to me."

"I did love you; but I never loved you half so well as I ought, Susy; and I never was worthy of you. Susy, I tell you—I tell you—my heart is breaking for your sake. It would have been well for both of us we had never seen, or known, or loved each other; for I know by my own heart what you must suffer."

"Denis, don't be cast down on my account; before I ever thought of you, when I was runnin' about the glens here, a lonely little orphan, I was often sorry, without knowin' why. Sometimes I used to wonder at it, and search my mind to find out what occasioned it: but I never could. I suppose it was because I saw other girls, like myself, havin' their little brothers an' sisters to play with or because I had no mother's voice to call me night or mornin', or her bosom to lay my head on, if I was sick or tired. I suppose it was this. Many a time, Denis, even then, I knew what sorrow was, and I often thought that, come what would to others, there was sorrow before me. I now find I was right; but for all that, Denis, it's betther that we should give up one another in time, than be unhappy by my bein' the means of turning you from the ways and duties of God."

The simple and touching picture which she drew of her orphan childhood, together with the tone of resignation and sorrow which ran through all she said, affected Denis deeply.

"Susan," he replied, "I am much changed of late. The prospect before me is a dark one—a mysterious one. It is not many months since my head was dizzy with the gloomy splendor which the pomps and ceremonies of the Church—soon, I trust, to be restored in this country to all her pride and power—presented to my imagination. But I have mingled with those on whom before this—that is, during my boyhood—I looked with awe, as on men who held vested in themselves some mysterious and spiritual power. I have mingled with them, Susan, and I find them neither better nor worse than those who still look upon them as I once did."

"Well, but, Denis, how does that bear upon your views?"

"It does, Susan. I said I have found them neither better nor worse than their fellow-creatures; but I believe they are not so happy. I think I could perceive a gloom, even in their mirth, that told of some particular thought or care that haunted them like a spirit. Some of them and not a few, in the moments of undisguised feeling, dissuaded me against ever entering the Church."

"I am sure they're happy," said Susan. "Some time ago, accordin' to your own words, you thought the same; but something has turned your heart from the good it was fixed upon. You're in a dangerous time, Denis; and it's not to be wondhered at, if the temptations of the devil should thry you now, in hopes to turn you from the service of God. This is a warnin' to me, too, Denis. May Heaven above forbid that I should be made the means of temptin' you from the duty that's before you!"

"No, Susan, dear, it's not temptation, but the fear of temptation, that prevails with me."

"But, Denis, surely if you think yourself not worthy to enter that blessed state, you have time enough to avoid it."

"Ay, but, Susy, there is the difficulty. I am now so placed that I can hardly go back. First, the disgrace of refusing to enter the Church would lie upon me as if I had committed a crime. Again, I would break my father's and my mother's heart: and rather than do that, I could almost submit to be miserable for life. And finally, I could not live in the family, nor bear the indignation of my brothers and other relations. You know, Susan, as well as I do, the character attached to those who put their friends to the expense of educating them for the Church, who raise their hopes and their ambition, and afterwards disappoint them."

"I know it."

"This, Susan, dear, prevails with me. Besides, the Church now is likely to rise from her ruins. I believe that if a priest did his duty, he might possibly possess miraculous power. There is great pomp and splendor in her ceremonies, a sense of high and boundless authority in her pastors; there is rank in her orders sufficient even for ambition. Then the deference, the awe, and the humility with which they are approached by the people—ah! Susan, there is much still in the character of a priest for the human heart to covet. The power of saying mass, of forgiving sin, of relieving the departed spirits of the faithful in another world, and of mingling in our holy sacrifices, with the glorious worship of the cherubims, or angels, in heaven—all this is the privilege of a priest, and what earthly rank can be compared to it?"

"None at all, Denis—none at all. Oh, think this way still, and let no earthly temptation—no—don't let—even me—what am I?—a poor humble girl—oh! no, let nothing keep you back from this."

The tears burst from her eyes, however, as she spoke.

"But, Denis," she added, "there is one thing that turns my brain. I fear that, even afther your ordination, I couldn't look upon you as I would upon another man. Oh, my heart would break if one improper thought of it was fixed upon you then."

"Susy, hear me. I could give up all, but you. I could bear to disappoint father, mother, and all; but the thought of giving you up for ever is terrible. I have been latterly in a kind of dream. I have been among friends and relatives until my brain was turned; but now I am restored to myself, and I find I cannot part with you. I would gladly do it; but I cannot. Oh, no, Susan, dear, my love for you was dimmed by other passions; but it was not extinguished. It now burns stronger and purer in my heart than ever. It does—it does. And, Susan, I always loved you."

Susan paused for some time, and unconsciously plucked a wild flower which grew beside her: she surveyed it a moment, and exclaimed:—

"Do you see this flower, Denis? it's a faded primrose. I'm like that flower in one sense; I'm faded; my heart's broke."

"No, my beloved Susan, don't say so; you're only low-spirited. Why should your heart be broke, and you in the very bloom of youth and beauty?"

"Do you remember our last meetin', Denis? Oh, how could you be so cruel then as to bid me think of marryin' another, as if I had loved you for anything but yourself? I'm but a simple girl, Denis, and know but little of the world; but if I was to live a thousand years, you would always see the sorrow that your words made me feel visible upon my countenance. I'm not angry with you, Denis; but I'm telling you the truth."

"Susan, my darling, this is either weakness of mind or ill health. I will see you as beautiful and happy as ever. For my part, I now tell you, that no power on earth can separate us! Yes, my beloved Susan, I will see you as happy and happier than I have ever seen you. That will be when you are my own young and guileless wife."

"Ah, no, Denis! My mind is made up: I can never be your wife, Do you think that I would bring the anger of God upon myself, by temptin' you back from the holy office you're entering into? Think of it yourself Denis. Your feelings are melted now by our discoorse, and, maybe, because I'm near you; but when time passes, you'll be glad that in the moment of weakness you didn't give way to them. I know it's natural for you to love me now. You're lavin' me—you're lavin' the place where I am—the little river and the glen where we so often met, and where we often spent many a happy hour together. That has an effect upon you; for why should I deny it—you see it—it is hard—very hard—even upon myself."

She neither sobbed nor cried so as to be heard, but the tears gushed down her cheeks in torrents.

"Susan," said Denis, in an unsteady voice, "you speak in vain. Every word you say tells me that I cannot live without you; and I will not."

"Don't say that, Denis. Suppose we should be married, think of what I would suffer if I saw you in poverty or distress, brought on because you married me! Why, my heart would sink entirely under it. Then your friends would never give me a warm heart. Me! they would never give yourself a, warm heart; and I would rather be dead than see you brought to shame, or ill-treatment, or poverty, on my account. Pray to God, Denis, to grant you grace to overcome whatever you feel for me. I have prayed both for you and myself. Oh, pray to him, Denis, sincerely, that he may enable you to forget that such, a girl—such an unhappy girl—as Susan Connor ever lived!"

Poor Denis was so much overcome that he could not restrain his tears. He gazed upon the melancholy countenance of the fair girl, in a delirium of love and admiration; but in a few minutes he replied:—

"Susan, your words are lost: I am determined. Oh! great heavens! what a treasure was I near losing! Susan, hear me: I will bear all that this world can inflict; I will bear shame, ill-treatment, anger, scorn, and every harsh word that may be uttered against me; I will renounce church, spiritual power, rank, honor; I will give up father and family—all—all that this world could flatter mo with: yes, I will renounce each and all for your sake! Do not dissuade me; my mind is fixed, and no power on earth can change it."

"Yes, Denis," she replied calmly, "there is a power, and a weak power, too, that will change it; for I will change it. Don't think, Denis, that in arguin' with you, against the feelin's of my own heart, I am doin' it without sufferin'. Oh, no, indeed! You know, Denis, I am a lonely girl; that I have neither brother, nor sister, nor mother to direct me. Sufferin'!—Oh, I wish you knew it! Denis, you must forget me. I'm hopeless now: my heart, as I said, is broke, and I'm strivin' to fix it upon a happier world! Oh! if I had a mother or a sister, that I could, when my breast is likely to burst, throw myself in their arms, and cry and confess all I feel! But I'm alone, and must bear all my own sorrows. Oh, Denis! I'm not without knowin' how hard the task is that I have set to myself. Is it nothing to give up all that the heart is fixed upon? Is it nothing to walk about this glen, and the green fields, to have one's eyes upon them, and to remember what happiness one has had in them, knowin', at the same time, that it's all blasted? Oh, is it nothing to look upon the green earth itself, and all its beauty—to hear the happy songs and the joyful voices of all that are about us—the birds singing sweetly, the music of the river flowin'—to see the sun shinin', and to hear the rustlin' of the trees in the warm winds of summer—to see and hear all this, and to feel that a young heart is brakin', or already broken within us—that we are goin' to lave it all—all we loved—and to go down into the clay under us? Oh, Denis, this is hard;—bitter is it to me, I confess it; for something tells me it will be my fate soon!"

"But, Susan"—

"Hear me out. I have now repated what I know I must suffer—what I know I must lose. This is my lot, and I must bear it. Now, Denis, will you grant your own Susan one request?"

"If it was that my life should save yours, I would grant it."

"It's the last and only one I will ever ask of you. My health has been ill, Denis; my strength is gone, and I feel I am gettin' worse every day: now when you hear that I am—that I am—gone,—will you offer up the first mass you say for my pace and rest in another world? I say the first, for you know there's more virtue in a first mass than in any other. Your Susan will be then in the dust, and you may feel sorrow, but not love for her."

"Never, Susan! For God's sake, forbear! You will drive me distracted. As I hope to meet judgment, I think I never loved you till now; and by the same oath, I will not change my purpose in making you mine."

"Then you do love me still, Denis? And you would give up all for your Susan? Answer me truly, for the ear of God is open to our words and thoughts."

"Then, before God, I love you too strongly for words to express; and I would and will give up all for your sake!"

Susan turned her eyes upon vacancy; and Denis observed that a sudden and wild light broke from them, which alarmed him exceedingly. She put her open hand upon her forehead, as if she felt pain, and remained glancing fearfully around her for a few minutes; her countenance, which became instantly like a sheet of paper, lost all its intelligence, except, perhaps, what might be gleaned from a smile of the most ghastly and desolating misery.

"Gracious heaven! Susan, dear, what's the matter? Oh, my God! your face is like marble! Dearest Susan, speak to me!—Oh, speak to me, or I will go distracted!"

She looked upon him long and steadily; but he perceived with delight that her consciousness was gradually returning. At length she drew a deep sigh, and requested him to listen.

"Denis," said she, "you must now be a man. We can never be married. I am PROMISED TO ANOTHER!"

"Promised to another! Your brain is turned, Susy. Collect yourself, dearest, and think of what you say."

"I know what I say—I know it too well! What did I say? Why—why," she added, with an unsettled look, "that I'm promised to another! It is true—true as God's in heaven. Oh, Denis! why did you lave me so' long without seein' me? I said my heart was broke, and you will soon know that it has bitter, bitter rason to be so. See here."

She had, during her reply, taken from her bosom a small piece of brown cloth, of a square shape, marked with the letters I. M. I. the initials of the names of Jesus, Mary, and Joseph. She kissed it fervently as she spoke, and desired Denis to look upon it and hear her.

"When you saw me last," she continued, "I left you in anger, because I thought you no longer loved me. Many a scaldin' tear I shed that nobody witnessed; many a wringin' my heart felt since that time. I got low, and, as I said, my health left me. I began to think of what I ought to do; and bein' so much' alone, my thoughts were never off it. At last I remembered the Virgin Mother of God, as bein' once a woman, and the likelier to pity one of her own kind in sorrow. I then thought of a scapular; and made a promise to myself, that if you didn't come within a certain time, I would dedicate myself to her for ever. I saw that you neglected me, and I heard so much of the way you spent your time, how you were pleasant and merry while my heart was breakin', that I made a vow to remain a spotless virgin all my life. I got a scapular, too, that I might be strengthened to keep my holy promise; for you didn't come to me within the time. This is it in my hand. It is now on me. The VOW IS MADE AND I AM MISERABLE FOB EVER!"

Denis sobbed and wrung his hands, whilst tears, intensely bitter, fell from his eyes.

"Oh, Susan!" he exclaimed, "what have you done? Miserable! Oh you have ruined me utterly! You have rendered us both for ever miserable!"

"Miserable!" she exclaimed with flashing eyes. "Who talks of misery?" But again she put her hand to her forehead, and endeavored to recollect herself. "Denis," she added, "Denis, my brain is turning! Oh, I have no friend! Oh, mother, that I never seen, but as if it was in a dream; mother, daughter of your daughter's heart, look down from heaven, and. pity your orphan child in her sore trouble and affliction! Oh, how often did I miss you, mother darlin', durin' all my life! In sickness I had not your tend her hands about me; in sorrow I could no' hear your voice; and in joy and happiness you were never with me to share them! I had not your advice, my blessed mother, to guide and direct me, to tache me what was right and what was wrong! Oh, if you will not hear your own poor lonely orphan, who will you hear? if you will not assist her, who ought you to assist? for, as sure as I stand here this night, you are a blessed saint in heaven. But let me not forget the Virgin Queen of Heaven, that I am bound to. I kneel to you, Hope of the Afflicted! To you let them go that have a broken heart, as I have! Queen of Glory, pity me!—Star of the Sea—Comfort of the Hopeless—Refuge of Sinners, hear me, strengthen and support me! And you will, too. Who did you ever cast away, mild and beautiful Virgin of Heaven? As the lily among thorns, so are you among the daughters of Adam![7] Yes, Denis, she will support me—she will support me! I feel her power on me now! I see the angels of heaven about her, and her mild countenance smilin' sweetly upon the broken flower! Yes, Denis, her glory is upon me!" The last words were uttered with her eyes flashing wildly as before, and her whole person and countenance evidently under the influence of a highly excited enthusiasm, or perhaps a touch of momentary insanity.

Poor Denis stood with streaming eyes, incapable of checking or interrupting her. He had always known that her education and understanding were above the common; but he never anticipated from her such capacity for deep feeling, united to so much vivacity of imagination as she then displayed. Perhaps he had not philosophy enough, at that period of his youth, to understand the effects of a solitary life upon a creature full of imagination and sensibility. The scenery about her father's house was wild, and the glens singularly beautiful; Susan lived among them alone, so that she became in a manner enamored of solitude; which, probably mote than anything else, gives tenderness to feeling and force to the imaginative faculties. Soon after she had pronounced the last words, however, her good sense came to her aid.

"Denis," said she, "you have seen my weakness; but you must now see my strength. You know we have a trial to go through before we part for ever."

"Oh! Susy, don't say 'for ever.' You know that the vow you made was a rash vow. It may be set aside."

"It was not a rash vow, Denis. I made it with a firm intention of keepin' it, and keep it I will. The Mother of God is not to be mocked, because I am weak, or choose to prefer my own will to hers."

"But, Susy, the Church can dissolve it. You know she has power to bind and to loose. Oh, for God's sake, Susy, if you ever loved me, don't attempt to take back your promise."

"I love you too well to destroy you, Denis. I will never stand between you and God, for that would be my crime. I will never bring disgrace, or shame, or poverty, upon you; for surely these things would fall upon you as a punishment for desartin' him. If you were another—if you weren't intended to be the servant of God, I could beg with you—starve with you—die with you. But when I am gone, remember, that I gave up all my hopes, that you might succeed in yours.

---

[7] The form of the Service of the Virgin, from which most of the above expressions are taken is certainly replete with beauty and poetry.

I'm sure that is love. Now, Denis, we must return our promises, the time is passin', and we'll both be missed from home."

"Susan, for the sake of my happiness, both in this world and in the next, don't take away all hope. Make me not miserable and wretched; send me not into the church a hypocrite. If you do, I will charge you with my guilt; I will charge you with the crimes of a man who will care but little what he does."

"You will have friends, Denis; pious men, who will direct you and guide you and wean your heart from me and the world. You will soon bless me for this. Denis," she added, with a smile of unutterable misery, "my mind is made up. I belong now to the Virgin Mother of God. I never will be so wicked as to forsake her for a mortal. If I was to marry you—with a broken vow upon me, I could not prosper. The curse of God and of his Blessed Mother would follow us both."

Denis felt perfectly aware of the view entertained by Susan, respecting such a vow as she had taken. To reason with her, was only to attack a prejudice which scorned reason. Besides this, he was not himself altogether free from the impression of its being a vow too solemn to be broken without the sanction of the Church.

"Let us go," said Susan, "to the same spot where we first promised. It was under this tree, in this month, last year. Let us give it back there."

The hand-promise in Ireland between the marriageable young of both sexes, is considered the most solemn and binding of all obligations. Few would rely upon the word or oath of any man who had been known to break a hand-promise. And, perhaps, few of the country girls would marry or countenance the addresses of a yoking person known to have violated such a pledge. The vow is a solemn one, and of course, given by mutual consent, by mutual consent, also, must it be withdrawn, otherwise, it is considered still binding. Whenever death removes one of the parties, without the other having had an opportunity of "giving it back," the surviving party comes, and in the presence of witnesses first grasping the hand of the deceased, repeats the form of words usual in withdrawing it. Some of these scenes are very touching and impressive, particularly one which the author had an opportunity of witnessing. It is supposed that in cases of death, if the promise be not thus dissolved, the spirit of the departed returns and haunts the survivor until it be cancelled.

When Denis and Susan had reached the hawthorn, they both knelt down. So exhausted, however, had Susan been by the agitation of her feelings, that Denis was under the necessity of assisting her to the place. He could perceive, too, that, amid the workings of her religious enthusiasm, she trembled like an aspen leaf.

"Now," said she, "you are stronger than I am, begin and repeat the words; I will repeat them with you."

"No," replied Denis, "I will never begin. I will never be the first to seal both your misery and mine."

"I am scarcely able," said she; "dear Denis, don't ask me to do what I have not strength for. But it's useless," she added; "you will never begin unless I do."

They then blessed themselves after the form of their church, and as they extended their right hands to each other, the tears fell fast from the eyes of both. The words they repeated were the same, with the difference of the name only.

"I, Susan Connor, in the presence of God, do release you, Denis O'Shaughnessy, from your promise of marriage to me, and from all promises of marriage that you ever made me. I now give you back that promise of marriage, and all promises of marriage you ever made me. To which I call God to witness."

Denis repeated the same words, substituting the name of Susan Connor.

The sobs of Susan were loud and incessant, even before she had concluded the words; their eyes were fixed upon each other with a hopeless and agonizing expression: but no sooner were they uttered, than a strong hysteric sense of suffocation rose to her throat; she panted rapidly for breath; Denis opened his arms, and she fell, or rather threw herself, over in a swoon upon his bosom. To press his lips to hers, and carry her to the brink of the well, was but the work of a moment. There he laid her, and after having sprinkled her face with water, proceeded to slap the palms of her hands, exclaiming,—

"Susan, my beloved, will you not hear me? Oh, look upon me, my heart's dearest treasure, and tell me that you're living. Gracious God! her heart is broken—she is dead! This—this—is the severest blow of all! I have killed her!"

She opened her eyes as he spoke, and Denis, in stooping to assist her, weeping at the same time like a child; received—a bang from a cudgel that made his head ring.

"Your sowl to the divil, you larned vagabone," said her father, for it was he, "is this the way you're preparin' yourself for the church? Comin' over that innocent colleen of a daughter o' mine before you set out," he added, taking Denis a second thwack across the shoulders—"before you set out for Maynewth!!"

"Why, you miserable vulgarian," said Denis, "I scorn you from the head to the heel. Desist, I say," for the father was about to lay in another swinger upon his kidney—"desist, I say, and don't approximate, or I will entangle the ribs of you!"

"My sowl to glory," said the father, "if ever I had a greater mind to ate my dinner, than I have to anoint you wid this cudgel, you black-coated skamer!"

"Get out, you barbarian," replied Denis, "how dare you talk about unction in connection with a cudgel? Desist, I say, for I will retaliate, if you approximate an inch. Desist, or I will baptize you in the well as Philip did the Ethiopian, without a sponsor. No man but a miserable barbarian would have had the vulgarity to interrupt us in the manner you did. Look at your daughter's situation!"

"The hussy," replied the father, "it's the supper she ought to have ready, instead of coortin' wid sich a larned vag——Heavens above me! What ails my child? Susy! Susy, *alanna dhas!* what's over you? Oh, I see how it is," he continued—"I see how it is! This accounts for her low spirits an' bad health for some time past! Susy, rouse yourself, avourneen! Sure I'm not angry wid you! My sowl to glory, Denis Shaughnessy, but you have broke my child's heart, I doubt!"

"Owen," said Denis, "your indecorous interruption has stamped you with the signature of genuine ignorance and vulgarity; still, I say, we must have some conversation on that subject immediately. Yes, I love your daughter a thousand times better than nay own life."

"Faith, I'll take care that we'll have discoorse about it," replied the father. "If you have been a villain to the innocent girl—if you have, Denny, why you'll meet your God sooner than you think. Mark my words. I have but one life, and I'll lose it for her sake, if she has come to ill."

"Here,", said Denis, "let me sprinkle her face with this cool water, that we may recover her, if possible. Your anger and your outrage, Owen, overcame the timid creature. Speak kindly to her, she is recovering. Thank God, she is recovering."

"Susy, avourneen," said the father, "rouse yourself,' ma colleen; rouse yourself, an' don't thrimble that way. The sorra one o' me's angry wid you, at all at all."

"Oh, bring me home," said the poor girl. "Father, dear, have no bad opinion of me. I done nothing, an' I hope I never will do anything, that would bring the blush of shame to your face."

"That's as true as that God's in heaven," observed Denis. "The angels in his presence be not purer than she is."

"I take her own word for it," said the father; "a lie, to the best of my knowledge, never came from her lips."

"Let us assist her home," said Denis. "I told you that we must have some serious conversation about her. I'll take one arm, and do you take the other."

"Do so," said the father, "an', Denny, as you're the youngest and the strongest, jist take up that pitcher o' wather in your hand, an' carry it to the house above."

Denis, who was dressed in his best black from top to toe, made a wry face or two at this proposal. He was able, however, for Susan's sake, to compromise his dignity: so looking about him, to be certain that there was no other person observing them, he seized the pitcher in one hand, gave Susan his arm, and in this unheroic manner assisted to conduct her home.

In about half an hour or better after this, Denis and Owen Connor proceeded in close and earnest conversation towards old Shaughnessy's. On entering, Denis requested to speak with his father and brothers in private.

"Father," said he, "this night is pregnant—that is, *vulgariter*, in the family way—with my fate."

"Throth, it is, avick. Glory be to Goodness!"

"Here is Owen Connor, an honest, dacent neighbor—"

"Throth, he is an honest, dacent man, said the lather, interrupting him.

"Yes," replied the son, "I agree with you. Well, he has a certain disclosure or proposal to make, which you will be pleased to take into your most serious consideration. I, for my part, cannot help being endowed with my own gifts, and if I happen to possess a magnet to attract feminine sensibility, it is to heaven I owe it, and not to myself."

"It is,"—said the father, "glory be to his name!"

"Don't be alarmed, or surprised, or angry, at anything Owen Connor may say to you. I speak significantly. There are perplexities in all human events, and the cardinal hinge of fate is forever turning. Now I must withdraw; but in, the meantime I will be found taking a serenade behind the garden, if I am wanted."

"Brian," said the father, "get the bottle; we can't on this night, any way, talk to Owen Connor, or to anybody else, wid dhry lips."

The bottle was accordingly got, and Owen, with no very agreeable anticipations, found himself compelled to introduce a very hazardous topic.

Denis, as he said, continued to walk to and fro behind the garden. He thought over the incidents of the evening, but had no hope that Owen Connor's proposal would be accepted. He knew his father and family too well for that. With respect to Susan's vow, he felt certain that any change of opinion on her part was equally improbable. It was clear, then, that he had no pretext for avoiding Maynooth; and as the shame, affliction, and indignation of the family would, he knew, be terrible, he resolved to conform himself to his circumstances, trusting to absence for that diminution of affection which it often produces. Having settled these points in his mind, he began to grope that part of his head which had come in contact with Owen Connor's cudgel. He had strong surmises that a bump existed, and on examining, he found that a powerful organ of self-esteem had been created.

At this moment he saw Owen Connor running past him at full speed, pursued by his father and brothers, the father brandishing a cudgel in his hand. The son, who understood all, intercepted the pursuers, commanding them, in a loud voice to stop. With his brothers he succeeded; but the father's wrath was not to be appeased so easily. Nothing now remained but to stand in his way, and arrest him by friendly violence; Denis, therefore, seized him, and, by assuming all his authority, at length prevailed upon him to give over the chase.

"Only think of him," exclaimed the father, breathless—"only think of him havin' the assurance to propose a match between you an' his baby-faced daughter! Ho! *Dher manhim*, Owen Connor," he shouted, shaking the staff at Owen as he spoke—"*Dher manhim!* if I was near you, I'd put your bones through other, for darin' to mintion sich a thing!"

Owen Connor, on finding that he was na longer pursued, stood to reconnoitre the enemy:—

"Denis Oge," he shouted back, "be on to Maynooth as fast as possible, except you wish to have my poor child left fatherless entirely. Go way, an' my blessin' be along wid you; but let there be never another word about that business while you live."

"Father," said Denis, "I'm scandalized at your conduct on this dignified occasion. I am also angry with Brian and the rest of you. Did you not observe that the decent man was advanced in liquor? I would have told you so at once, were it not that he was present while I spoke. Did I not give you as strong a hint as possible? Did I not tell you that 'I spoke significantly?' Now hear me. Take the first opportunity of being reconciled to Owen Connor. Be civil to him; for I assure you he esteems me very highly. Be also kind to his daughter, who is an excellent girl; but I repeat it, her father esteems me highly."

"Does he think highly of you, Denis?"

"I have said so," he replied.

"Then, throth, we're sorry for what has happened, poor man. But the never a one o' me, Denis, saw the laste sign of liquor about him. Throth, we will make it up wid him, thin. An' we'll be kind to his daughter, too, Denis."

"Then as a proof that you will follow my advice, I lay it on you as a duty, to let me know how they are, whenever you write to me."

"Throth, we will, Denis;—indeed will we. Come in now, dear; this is the last night you're to be wid us, an' they're all missin! you in the house."

On that night no person slept in Denis O'Shaughnessy's, except our hero, and his mother and sisters. As morning approached a heaviness of spirits prevailed among the family, which of course was not felt by any except his immediate relations. The more distant friends, who remained with them for the night, sang and plied the bottle with a steadiness which prevented them from feeling the want of rest. About six o'clock, breakfast was ready, Denis dressed, and every arrangement made for his immediate departure. His parents—his brothers, and his sisters were all in tears, and he himself could master his emotions with great difficulty. At length the hour to which the family of our candidate had long looked forward, arrived, and Denis rose to depart for Maynooth. Except by the sobs and weeping, the silence was unbroken when he stood up to bid them farewell.

The first he embraced was his eldest brother, Brian: "Brian," said he, but he could not proceed—his voice failed him: he then extended his hand, but Brian clasped him in tis arms—kissed his beloved brother, and wept with strong grief; even then there was not a dry eye in the house. The parting with his other brothers was equally tender—they wept loudly and bitterly, and Denis joined in their grief. Then came his sisters, who, one by one, hung upon him, and sobbed as if he had been dead. The grief of his youngest sister, Susan, was excessive. She threw her arms about his neck, and said she would not let him go; Denis pressed her to his heart, and the grief which he felt, seemed to penetrate his very soul.

"Susan," said he, "Susan, may the blessing of God rest upon you till I see you again!"—and the affectionate girl was literally torn from his arms.

But how came the most affecting part of the ceremony. His parents had stood apart—their hands locked in each other, both in tears, whilst he took leave of the rest. He now approached his mother, and reverently kneeling down, implored in words scarcely intelligible, her blessing and forgiveness; he extended both his hands—"Mother," he added, "I ask—humbly and penitently, I ask your blessing; it will be sweet to me from your beloved lips, dear mother;—pardon me if I ever—as I feel I often did—caused you a pang of sorrow by my disobedience and folly. Oh, pardon me—pardon me for all now! Bless your son, kindest of mothers, with your best and tenderest blessing!"

She threw herself in his arms, and locking him in her embrace, imprinted every part of his face with kisses. "Oh, Denis," she exclaimed, "there is but one more who will miss you more nor I will—Oh, my darlin' son—our pride—our pride—our heart's pride—our honor, and our credit! Sure, *anim machree*, I have nothin' to forgive you for, my heart's life; but may the blessin' of God and of a happy mother light on you! And, Denis *asthore*, wasn't it you that made me happy, and that made us all happy. May my blessin' and the blessin' of God rest upon you—keep you from every evil, and in every good, till my eyes will be made glad by lookin' on you agin!"

A grief more deep, and a happiness more full, than had yet been felt, were now to come forth. Denis turned to his father—his companion in many a pastime, and in many a walk about their native fields. In fair—in market—at mass—and at every rustic amusement within their reach—had he been ever at the side of that indulgent father, whose heart and soul were placed in him. Denis could not utter a word, but kept his streaming eyes fixed upon the old man, with that yearning expression of the heart which is felt when it desires to be mingled with the very existence of the object that it loves. Old Denis advanced, under powerful struggles, to suppress his grief; he knelt, and, as the tears ran in silence down his cheeks, thus addressed himself to God:—

"I kneel down before you, oh, my God a poor sinner! I kneel here in your blessed presence, with a heart—with a happy heartens day, to return you thanks in the name of myself and the beloved partner you have given me through the cares and thrials of this world, to give you our heart's best thanks for graciously permittin' us to see this day! It is to you we owe it, good Father of Heaven! It is to you we owe this—an' him—my heart's own son, that kneels before me to be blessed by my lips! Yes—yes, he is—he is the pride of our lives!—He is the mornin' star among us! he was ever a good son; and you know that from the day he was born to this minute, he never gave me a sore heart! Take him under your own protection! Oh, bless him as we wish, if it be your holy will to do so!—Bless him and guard him, for my heart's in him: it is—he knows it—everybody knows it;—and if anything was to happen him——"

He could proceed no further: the idea of losing his son, even in imagination, overpowered him;—he rose, locked him to his breast, and for many minutes the grief of both was loud and vehement.

Denis's uncle now interposed: "The horses," said he, "are at the door, an' time's passin'."

"Och, thrue for you, Barny," said old Denis; "come, *acushla*, an' let me help you on your horse. We will go on quickly, as we're to meet Father Finnerty at the crass-roads."

Denis then shook hands with them all, not forgetting honest Phadrick Murray, who exclaimed, as he bid him farewell, "Arrah! Misther Denis, aroon, won't you be thinkin' of me now an' thin in the College? Faix, if you always argue as bravely wid the Collegians as you did the day you proved me to be an ass you'll soon be at the head of them!"

"Denis," said the uncle, "your father excuses me in regard of havin' to attend my cattle in the fair to-day. You won't be angry wid me, dear, for lavin' you now, as my road lies this other way. May the blessin' of God and his holy mother keep you till I see you agin! an', Denis, if you'd send me a scrape or two, lettin' me know what a good parish 'ud be worth; for I intend next spring to go wid little Barny to the Latin!"

This Denis promised to do; and after bidding him farewell, he and his friends—some on horseback and numbers on foot—set out on their journey; and as they proceeded through their own neighborhood, many a crowd was collected to get a sight of Denis O'Shaughnessy going to Maynooth.

It was one day in autumn, after a lapse of about two years, that the following conversation took place between a wealthy grazier from the neighboring parish, and one of our hero's most intimate, acquaintances. It is valuable only as it throws light upon Denis's ultimate situation in life, which, after all, was not what our readers might be inclined to expect.

"Why, then, honest man," said Denis's friend, "that's a murdherin' fine dhrove o' bullocks you're bringin' to the fair?"

"Ay!" replied the grazier, "you may say that. I'm thinkin' it wouldn't be asay to aquil them."

"Faix, sure enough. Where wor they fed, wid simmision?"

"Up in Teernahusshogue. Arrah, will you tell me what weddin' was that that passed awhile agone?"

"A son of ould Denis O'Shaughnessy's, God be merciful to his sowl!"

"Denis O'Shaughnessy! Is it him they called the 'Pigeon-house?' An' is it possible he's dead?"

"He's dead, nabor, an' in throth, an honest man's dead!"

"As ever broke the world's bread. The Lord make his bed in heaven this day! Hasn't he a son larnin' to be a priest in May-newth?"

"Ah! *Fahreer gairh!* That's all over."

"Why, is he dead, too?"

"Be Gorra, no—but the conthrairy to that. 'Twas his weddin' you seen passin' a minute agone."

"Is it the young sogarth's? Musha, bad end to you, man alive, an' spake out. Tell us how that happened. Sowl it's a quare business, an' him was in Maynewth!"

"Faith, he was so; an' they say there wasn't a man in Maynewth able to tache him. But, passin' that over—you see, the father, ould Denis—an' be Gorra, he was very bright, too, till the son grewn up, an' drownded him wid the languidges—the father, you see, ould Denis himself, tuck a faver whin the son was near a year in the college, an' it proved too many for him. He died; an' whin young Dinny hard of it, the divil a one of him would stay any longer in Maynewth. He came home like a scarecrow, said he lost his health in it, an' refused to go back. Faith, it was a lucky thing that his father died beforehand, for it would brake his heart. As it was, they had terrible work about it. But ould Denis is never dead while young Denis is livin'. Faix, he was as stiff as they wor stout, an' wouldn't give in; so, afther ever so much' wranglin', he got the upper hand by tellin' them that he wasn't able to bear the college at all; an' that if he'd go back to it he'd soon folly his father."

"An' what turned him against the college? Was that thrue?"

"Thrue!—thrue indeed! The same youth was never at a loss for a piece of invintion whin it sarved him. No, the sarra word of thruth at all was in it. He soodered an' palavered a daughter of Owen Connor's, Susy—all the daughter he has, indeed—before he wint to Maynewth at all, they say. She herself wasn't for marryin' him, in regard of a vow she had; but there's no doubt but he made her fond of him, for he has a tongue that 'ud make black white, or white black, for that matter. So, be Gorra, he got the vow taken off of her by the Bishop; she soon recovered her health, for she was dyin' for love of him, an'—you seen their weddin'. It 'ud be worth your while to go a day's journey to get a sight of her—she's allowed to be the purtiest girl that ever was in this part o' the counthry."

"Well! well! It's a quare world. An' is the family all agreeable to it now?"

"Hut! where was the use of houldin' out aginst him? I tell you, he'd make them agreeable to any thing, wanst he tuck it into his head. Indeed, it's he that has the great larnin' all out! Why, now, you'd hardly b'lieve me, when I tell you that he'd prove you to be an ass in three minutes; make it as plain as the sun. He would; an' often made an ass o' myself."

"Why, now that I look at you—aren't you Dan Murray's nephew?"

"Phadrick Murray, an' divil a one else, sure enough."

"How is your family, Phadrick? Why, man, you don't know your friends—my name's Cahill."

"Is it Andy Cahill of Phuldhu? Why, thin, death alive, Andy, how is every bit of you? Andy, I'm regulatin' everything at this weddin', an' you must turn over your horse till we have a dhrop for ould times. Bless my sowl! sure, I'd know your brother round a corner; an' yourself, too, I ought to know, only that I didn't see you since you wor a slip of a gorsoon. Come away, man, sure thim men o' yours can take care o' the cattle. You'll asily overtake thim."

"Throth, I don't care if I have a glass wid an ould friend. But, I hope your whiskey won't overtake me, Phadrick?"

"The never a fear of it, your father's son has too good a head for that. Ough! man alive, if you could stay for the weddin'! Divil a sich a let out ever was seen in the county widin the mimory of the ouldest man in it, as it'll be. Denis is the boy that 'ud have the dacent thing or nothin'."

The grazier and Phadrick Murray then bent their steps to Owen Connor's house, where the wedding was held. It is unnecessary to say that Phadrick plied his new acquaintance to some purpose. Ere two hours passed the latter had forgotten his bullocks as completely as if he had never seen them, and his drovers were left to their own discretion in effecting their sale. As for Andy Cahill, like many another sapient Irishman, he preferred his pleasure to his business, got drunk, and danced, and sung at Denis O'Shaughnessy's wedding, which we are bound to say was the longest, the most hospitable, and most frolicsome that ever has been remembered in the parish from that day to the present.

Echo Library
www.echo-library.com

Echo Library uses advanced digital print-on-demand technology to build and preserve an exciting world class collection of rare and out-of-print books, making them readily available for everyone to enjoy.

Situated just yards from Teddington Lock on the River Thames, Echo Library was founded in 2005 by Tom Cherrington, a specialist dealer in rare and antiquarian books with a passion for literature.

Please visit our website for a complete catalogue of our books, which includes foreign language titles.

The Right to Read

Echo Library actively supports the Royal National Institute of the Blind's Right to Read initiative by publishing a comprehensive range of large print and clear print titles.

Large Print titles are in 16 point Tiresias font as recommended by the RNIB.

Clear Print titles are in 13 point Tiresias font and designed for those who find standard print difficult to read.

Customer Service

If there is a serious error in the text or layout please send details to feedback@echo-library.com and we will supply a corrected copy. If there is a printing fault or the book is damaged please refer to your supplier.

Printed in the United Kingdom
by Lightning Source UK Ltd.
131411UK00001B/409/A